C OPYRIGHT © 2019/2021 BY GMS written as Tobey Alexander

All rights reserved. Cover design by Tobey Alexander / TAGS Creative Book design by Tobey Alexander.

No part of this book may be reproduced in any form or by any electronic or mechanical means including information storage and retrieval systems, without permission in writing from the author. The only exception is by a reviewer, who may quote short excerpts in a review.

Published using self-publishing services. All enquiries directed to the author visiting https://tobeyalexander.wixsite.com /tobeyalexander or www.tobey-alexander.com.This book is a work of fiction. Names, characters, places, and incidents either are products of the author's imagination or are used fictitiously. Any resemblance to actual persons, living or dead, events, or locales is entirely coincidental.

10 9 8 7 6 5 4

TIMOTHY SCOTT: SHADOW ISLAND

BEHIND THE MIRROR BOOK I

TOBEY ALEXANDER

TAGS CREATIVE

EXCLUSIVE FREE PREQUEL

DEDICATION

THIS STORY WAS BORN during an early-morning work-out and grown with the help of my sons as we climbed Ben Nevis. Climbing to the top of the United Kingdom aged 10 and 8 they corrected my ideas and between us we created a story I am proud to write. We are all unique, different and my bloodline is no different as I carry a rare genetic deletion we have only recently learned about. We wanted a hero that is as Unique and different as we are and I hope you too will adventure with us as we celebrate the difference in all of us.

WELCOME TO MIELIKUVITUS

Mielikuvitus

BRIGHTLANDS

Parrot City

Eternal Lake

Halo Cove

Mystic Forest

Rainbow River

Torn Mountains

The Narrows

Shadow Island

SHADOWLANDS

Faceless Cliffs

FORGOTTENLANDS

CHAPTER ONE

THE RECURRING DREAM

IT ALWAYS STARTED THE same way. The room was always dark, but far off there was the sound of water dripping somewhere in the distance. Although he had never seen what surrounded him, Timothy had always believed he was in a cave somewhere.

Although it was only a dream, a lucid and vivid one that felt all too real, Timothy could almost smell the dampness in the air. The *dripping* sound continued off in the distance and while he could hear that, he felt calm.

It was impossible for him to say how many nights he had found himself dragged from another dream into this pitch-black place. The first time, he had woken quickly from the dream drenched in sweat and gasping for breath. Now, however, he had stayed longer and longer until new things happened and the dream evolved into something else.

What started as a dream of darkness had soon become a nightmare, a nightmare he was now all too familiar with.

Timothy Scott had been having the same recurring dream for the last four years and with every year, it had got worse and worse. When he had first ventured into the dark and seen what hid in there, he had refused to sleep for days. His parents had tried everything to comfort him, but at nine, there had been nothing they could do to calm him.

Now, however, the dream had become almost familiar. It changed nothing about the terror that it brewed in his stomach, but with each exposure, it had become a more expected experience than a terrifying, inescapable nightmare.

Timothy had convinced himself, even in his slumber, that it was just a dream and he would, at some point, wake.

Yet today felt different.

The dripping water faded, and the sound of light footfalls started. Distantly at first, he knew what to expect. Even if he didn't know *who* was coming, he knew *what* was coming.

The footsteps grew louder, nearer, and as it did, the air grew colder and his breath condensed in front of his face. Timothy felt the hairs on the back of his neck stand on end, and he knew he wasn't alone.

'You come back again?'

The voice was only just above a whisper. Laced with a sinister hush, he searched the darkness for the source. Timothy could pinpoint nothing as the voice spoke again, this time somewhere close behind him.

'I see you walking in the dark, blind as always.'

Timothy spun but could still see nothing.

'Who are you?' he tried to ask, but his voice caught in his throat and his mouth moved without making a sound.

It was always the same feeling. No matter how hard he tried, he could not speak. Timothy tried to talk, then shout and scream, but he never made a sound. When he was silent, unable to speak or communicate was when the panic would set in. His heart would race and the world would feel it was closing in on him.

Tonight was no different. The panic began to simmer, and the darkness felt like it was closing in on him, wrapping around him like an unseen fog.

'You will never escape me, never escape this place.' The eerie voice hissed. 'You are destined to remain in the dark forever.'

The eyes.

Burning like fire-red in front of him, he could make out the snake-like slit pupils and nothing else. They appeared inches from his face and he always tried to pull away. But something held him in place. Unable to escape the burning fire eyes, Timothy could only stare as the voice continued to goad him.

'I see into your soul, you are not Partum. Stay safe where you are. If you come to me, it will be your end.'

The eyes burned brighter, growing in intensity until Timothy could feel the heat against his skin. A blood-curdling scream filled the air, and the eyes lurched at him.

As the burning fire touched his skin, Timothy sat bolt upright in bed grasping at his chest, lungs screaming for breath and body drenched in sweat.

'Leave me alone!' He hollered and felt relief as the words burst from his lips.

As Timothy fought to calm his racing heart, he saw the familiarity of his bedroom illuminated by his plug-in nightlight.

'Timothy?' His mum asked as she bathed his room in light. 'Are you ok?'

Sat-up in his bed, Timothy looked terrified and dishevelled. Dressed in his grey pyjamas, stained with sweat, his normally red hair appeared brown in the dim light. Eyes wide, he turned to look at his mum and started shaking.

'Take a deep breath.' His mother comforted and sat on the bed next to him.

She had always been able to calm him. It was her voice, he realised, the fact she always sounded soft and helped to slow his racing heart. No matter how many nights he disturbed her sleep, she would always come. She would wrap him in her arms until the dream had gone, and he was once again calm.

Resting his head on her shoulder, he wrapped his shaking arms around her and hugged her tight.

'Same dream?' She asked, and he answered with a nod against her shoulder. 'I wish there was something we could do to help.'

'Hey Little Man,' his dad chirped as he pulled a t-shirt over his head. 'Same thing?'

'Yeah,' Timothy answered, his voice still shaky.

'I know what'll help,' his dad offered a wink and smile before disappearing out of his room.

Timothy remained resting against his mum's shoulder until his dad came back holding a pint-glass filled with milk. Timothy took the glass and sat back against his headboard as he sipped the cold milk.

'You get back to bed,' his dad offered as his mum stood after kissing his head. 'I'll stay with him for a bit, then I'm sure we will be back to sleep in no time.'

Timothy watched as his mum and dad shared a quick hug and his mum left to return to her own bed. Once they were alone, his dad turned and looked at his son with a very mischievous grin.

'Want anything else to go with that?'

Before Timothy could answer, his dad pulled out an open packet of chocolate bourbon biscuits and emptied two out of the pack into his hand. With the same cheeky smile, his father took the last biscuit from the packet and ate it himself.

'Just don't tell your mum!' He winked and waited with Timothy until he had finished his drink and midnight biscuits.

There was one thing that Timothy had never shared with his parents about the nightmare. It never dawned on him until he was ready to settle again as they returned to their own room. Every time he had the nightmare, the first thing he remembered, when his mind had stopped racing, was the time displayed on his bedside clock.

Every time, without fail, the clock showed the same time: 03:10

As his dad turned out the light and Timothy laid his head on the pillow, he tried to understand what the time meant. As he mulled over the time, he heard a whisper in the corner of his room.

'Until next time,' the same voice from his dream hushed. 'Sleep well Timothy Scott.'

Dragging the quilt up over his head, Timothy clamped his eyes shut and held the material tight around his head.

By the time he fell asleep again, the voice had fallen silent, and he heard nothing more from the menacing fire-eyed nightmare.

CHAPTER TWO

A DOCTOR'S APPOINTMENT

T IMOTHY WAS NOT A fan of the doctor's waiting room. It had the same magazines now as it had almost a year ago when he had first been taken there by his parents. Leafing through the tattered pages of the same comic he had read every time, he sighed with frustration.

Aiden, his older brother, had taken great pleasure in pointing out the fact Timothy had once again woken the house with a bad dream. Before leaving for the doctor's appointment, his brother had offered the usual comments as they ate breakfast.

'Scared of the dark again, little bro?' He had giggled while stuffing his face with toast, spilling jam down his school uniform.

'Leave him alone Aiden.' His dad had warned him.

'I thought little kids were supposed to grow out of bad dreams.'

'Try being more supportive.' His mother had scorned as she moved to wipe the jam from his jumper. 'At least Timothy can eat his breakfast without spilling it down himself.'

The slight flush to his brother's cheeks made Timothy smile. The smile did not go unnoticed by Aiden, who, as he pushed past to change his top, offered one last whispered comment.

'Maybe you'll grow out of it one day *baby* brother.'

Checking to make sure his parents weren't listening, Aiden scurried out of the dining room and disappeared after to walk to school.

'Pay no attention to him,' his dad had comforted as they walked out to the car. 'Older brothers always have a way of picking the right things to say to upset us.'

'I know.' Timothy sighed and climbed into the car.

The journey had been quiet, nobody speaking in the car, and mostly Timothy looked out of the window as the world moved by.

There was always one advantage, in Timothy's mind, with hospital appointments. While he didn't like the constant questions and reliving his nightmares, it got him out of a morning at school and that was never a bad thing.

'Timothy?' The familiar voice announced as the doctor's office door opened.

There was something about Doctor Ingrid Live Timothy couldn't put his finger on. She was a very formal woman, aged in her forties, with a head of jet-black hair tied back in a tight ponytail. Her angular face looked stern, imposing and frigid, her bright-blue eyes looked ice-cold as she peered through the tinted lenses of her glasses. Her appearance had intimidated Timothy the first time they had met but, in this case her looks were very deceiving.

While there was something different about her, she had soon melted away his wariness and proved to be a warm woman who he had grown to trust with expressing himself and sharing his dreams.

'Good morning young man,' she always greeted him this way, and it almost made him feel like an adult. 'Do you want your parents in today?'

Timothy was under no illusion that his parents *had* to come into the appointment, but the mere fact Dr Live pretended to give him a choice meant a lot to him. Feigning a thoughtful look on his face, he tapped a finger on his chin for a moment before giving her an answer.

'I suppose they can,' he said as he turned to look at his parents. 'If they promise to behave themselves.'

'We will try,' his mum grinned and stood up to follow him into the doctor's office.

As his dad moved behind him, he ruffled his hand through Timothy's hair and suddenly the anxiety he had felt towards the appointment faded away.

'Have we had any more of these nightmares then, Timothy?' Dr Live asked as they took their seats around the grand oak desk in the middle of the room.

'Yes,' he answered sheepishly.

'When was the last one?'

'Last night.' He watched as she opened her notepad and started making notes.

Timothy had always found it strange that the doctor used a pen and paper. Even at school, the teachers used tablets and phones to make their notes, yet the doctor preferred a fountain pen and paper notebook. It was all old-fashioned and curious to him.

'Was it the same as last time or has anything changed?'

Timothy paused for a moment. Although he trusted Dr Live, he didn't feel he wanted to share the fact the voice had spoken to him after the nightmare, when he had been *awake*. Feeling the eyes of everyone on him, Timothy stopped thinking about the voice and answered the doctor.

'It's been the same since last time.' He lied. 'The dark room. I think it's a cave and the burning eyes.'

'Did you try reminding yourself that it was only a dream, like we practiced?'

'Yes,' Timothy's cheeks flushed. 'It didn't work though, it's like the nightmare knows and just makes me feel cold and alone. It's like the more I try to fight it, the colder it gets until all I can think about is the cold.'

'And what happens then?'

Timothy dropped his gaze as the memory of the burning eyes glaring at him filled his head. As he tensed with the image, he felt his mother's hand wrap around his clenched fingers.

'It's ok,' she hushed in his ear.

'The eyes talk to me and then,' he struggled to find the words. 'And then, they attack me and I wake up.'

'It's ok,' Dr Live comforted as she made her notes and placed the paper onto the desk. 'None of this is uncommon. We just need to help you cope with whatever is going on in your head, Timothy.'

The doctor rose from her seat and moved to a bookshelf on the far side of the room.

They spent the remainder of the appointment with Dr Live trying to explain to him what she thought may have been causing his vivid dreams. There were a lot of words he didn't understand and he could see by the concerned look on his mother's face that the terms the doctor was using were alien to him, but meant something to her.

After almost an hour, the appointment was over and Timothy had taken in a little of what they said. All he could think about were the burning eyes watching him in the darkness. So much so that his mother had to shake him from his daydream when the appointment was over.

'There should be a lot there for you to read through,' Dr Live explained as she handed his father a pile of pamphlets and printed sheets. 'You just need to remember that this isn't something we want to cure. There is nothing wrong with Timothy. He just

11

sees things different from how we do and we need to adjust to that.'

His mother wiped a tear from her eye as she shook the doctor's hand.

'Thank you so much for all you've done.'

'It's no problem at all.' Dr Live replied, the smile breaking through the icy exterior as she turned to talk to Timothy. 'As for you, Timothy, you need to always remember you are unique. There's nothing wrong with being different and if anyone tells you otherwise, then they are wrong. Do you understand that?'

Timothy nodded, but the doctor seemed unconvinced by his answer.

'We will get you through this, I promise. We have lots of little tricks to help people who see the world a little differently.'

'Thank you.'

The doctor moved around the table and dropped to her knee in front of him so she could whisper to him. Leaning in close, she spoke only loud enough for him to hear.

'The things you see and feel, Timothy, are yours and yours alone. They are your world and it is a magical place. We just need to find a way for you to realise you are strong enough to be in that world and not be afraid.'

Her words filled him with a strange sense of pride; all the things he feared about being different seemed inconsequential.

As they left the office, Timothy did not understand what had been said to his parents, but they were deep in adult conversation as they walked through the hospital to the car. Left alone with his thoughts, Timothy felt very much alone. He knew whatever the doctor had said would be a new line for his older brother to attack him with.

'There's nothing wrong with him,' his dad declared and once again ruffled his hair. 'He's our boy, and he's almost as mad as his old man!'

The worry of Aiden faded as he grabbed his dad and hugged him tight.

CHAPTER THREE

BROTHERLY LOVE

B Y THE TIME TIMOTHY returned home after a long lunch with his parents, it was too late to return to school. Hiding his pleasure at the news, Timothy busied himself with the Lego in his room for the rest of the afternoon.

Leaving his mum and dad alone, he soon forgot the appointment with Dr Live. Between adventures with the tiny figures in the castle he had constructed, Timothy lost all track of time. He had never found it difficult to imagine the adventures he played with his toys. More often than not, they could find him lost in the sea of his own imagination.

As he smashed the side wall of the castle into a dozen small pieces, the sound of the front door slamming shut snatched him back from his imagined battle.

'Aiden!' he gasped and looked around the shared playroom.

Although his brother was two years his senior, they still shared the playroom. Since moving to comprehensive school, their parents had moved a desk and computer into the room.

That aside, it remained as much a place to work as a play for the pair of them. The desk that Aiden used was in a mess and littered with bricks from the played out battle Timothy had been lost in.

'You'd better not be playing with my stuff, Tim.'

Timothy's heart raced as he dropped the small figures to the floor and hurried to tidy up the mess on the desk. No sooner had he scooped the first handful of bricks from the desk and chair did the door burst open and Aiden stormed through it.

'Didn't miss much at school,' Aiden chuckled as he tossed his schoolbag onto the desk in front of the window. 'Picked a good day to skive off.'

'I wasn't skiving,' Timothy defended as he dropped the Lego back into a basket beside the castle. 'I had to see the doctor again.'

'Oh, you're special head doctor.' Aiden laughed. 'Did they find your brain, or is it still missing?'

Aiden was not a nasty brother. He had always looked after Timothy, but he had his moments. As his brother unhooked the tie from around his neck and changed out of his uniform, Timothy just wanted to be alone. He was not in the mood for name-calling and jokes at his expense.

'Nothing to say?' Aiden pressed as he slipped a football shirt over his head. 'Oh well, I'm off to the field. I would ask you if

15

you wanted to come, but you're too busy playing with baby toys and your silly invisible friend.'

Aiden scooped a scuffed football from the floor and jogged back out of the room. It had been less than two minutes and already Timothy felt drained. As the door closed behind his brother, he breathed a sigh of relief.

'I'm not silly!'

The voice was familiar and Timothy felt a smile creep across his face.

'I never said you were. It was Aiden.'

'Oh, I know that.' The voice was tuneful, the words almost seemed to be sung as they were spoken. 'As far as big brothers go, he isn't too bad, but sometimes...'

'Yeah, sometimes he's a butt-head!'

Both the voice and Timothy chuckled at the name calling, and all the wariness of his exchange with Aiden wafted away.

The voice he heard belonged to his truest friend. Nobody else had ever heard the voice, and even Timothy had never seen the source. But he had been with him as long as Timothy could remember. The voice went by the name of Aleobe and Timothy had spent many of his loneliest hours in the darkness of night sharing every secret he had with his invisible friend.

His family had embraced his friendship with Aleobe when he had been younger. Parents, as they do, encouraged the friendship, but as he had grown older and still claimed to hear the voice, they had become more concerned.

It was, Timothy suspected, one thing his parents had discussed with Dr Live in one of the many appointments where he had been guided back to the waiting room to play with the hospital toys.

Aleobe was very much real to Timothy and nothing his brother, parents, or peers could say would ever convince him differently.

'You had the dream again last night, didn't you?' Aleobe quizzed, the voice sounding like whatever it came from was sat amongst the walls of the castle.

'Yeah,' Timothy shrugged and sat cross-legged, looking at the construction. 'Same as always, with the eyes.'

'But there was something else, wasn't there?'

'What do you mean?'

'After your dad gave you the biscuits, when he turned out the lights, there was something else wasn't there?'

Timothy looked around the room, sheepish, before turning back to the toy castle.

'I heard the voice again.'

'In your sleep?'

Timothy shook his head from side-to-side in answer.

'Did you see anything?' Aleobe pressed, his musical voice seeming to move closer to Timothy. 'Was there anything there when it spoke?'

'No, there wasn't anything, it was just the same voice in the corner of my room.'

'I'm sorry I wasn't there, in your dream with you.' Aleobe announced, his voice filled with apology. 'I wasn't by your side and I should have been.'

'It's ok,' Timothy defended. 'I'm big enough to look after myself. The doctor thinks I should be able to take control of the dreams soon.'

'I'm sure you could.' Aleobe whispered. 'If they were dreams.'

Timothy was about to ask what his friend meant when the door to his room burst open. Without warning, the football Aiden had taken with him was thrown against the far wall of the room. Aleobe fell silent and Aiden stormed into the room in a fit of anger and slumped into the chair in front of the desk.

'I can do it tomorrow before school!' Aiden bellowed through the open door.

'Homework before football, you know the rules.' Timothy heard his mother shout up the stairs.

'It's not fair!' Aiden barked, and slammed his hand onto the desk.

For a moment Timothy watched his older brother, who dramatically had buried his head into his crossed arms. It was at times like these that Aiden struggled to understand why his brother got so angry about things. It was, and always had been, a rule that homework had to be done before sports and clubs. The only exception to this was when Aiden had got a job after school delivering newspapers.

To Timothy rules were rules and unless he was right that something was out of line, then he would always follow them.

Aiden, however, would do all he could to push back and test his parent's limits. That always ended in the same situation, with Aiden sulking in the playroom or his bedroom and his parents barking in irritation when dinner was ready.

Sensing it was the right time to leave his brother alone to sulk, Timothy stood up and crept out of the room, leaving Aiden to sit defiantly at the desk staring out of the window over the top of his folded arms.

'Come on Aleobe, let's see what's for dinner.'

Closing the door behind him, Timothy made his way into the hall and walked down the wide staircase.

Reaching the bottom of the stairs, Timothy stopped and looked at the large mirror his father had mounted on the wall. It had been there as long as Timothy could remember, and he hated it. The mirror was an odd design, large and square, with a circle separating the mirrored glass into five sections. Two of the smaller sections were cracked, and they had never replaced the mirrors. That fact alone confused Timothy, but the wood was dark and the mirror had always caught his eye peculiarly.

Timothy had never been able to put his finger on it, but sometimes, only rarely, out of the corner of his eye, he would sense movement in the mirror. When he turned to look, there was always nothing but his reflection looking back at him.

Moving past the mirror with more haste than was necessary, he opened the door to the lounge and was greeted by the welcoming smell of pizza. Forgetting the mirror, he closed the door and for a moment all was once again normal in the house.

CHAPTER FOUR

THE MIRROR

TIMOTHY AVOIDED AIDEN FOR the rest of the evening and before long, the ritual of bedtime was upon him. As it was a Friday night, after his younger sister had been safely tucked into bed, the brothers were allowed to stay up a little later. Having watched a film and eaten far more sweets than they should have, Timothy could feel his eyes starting to close as he watched the last part of the film.

'Look who's getting tired.' His dad laughed from across the sofa.

'No, I'm fine.' Timothy argued and missed as he tried to put a piece of popcorn in his mouth.

Soon after the film finished, both Timothy and Aiden crawled up the stairs towards the bathroom to finish getting ready for bed. Their rooms were next to one another and had a connected bathroom between them. As he finished brushing his teeth, Aiden stopped his younger brother from opening the door into his bedroom.

'Make sure you don't wake us all up with another one of your silly dreams.' Aiden warned. 'Even Cathy is getting bored, and she's only eight.'

'I can't help it.' Timothy bit back in defence.

'Even your baby sister can sleep without nightmares,' Aiden mocked. 'Maybe you should take after her and grow up a bit.'

Timothy blushed with anger as his brother smirked at him before letting go of the handle allowing him into his bedroom. Rather than say anything, Timothy yanked the door open and stormed into his bedroom, leaving Aiden alone in the bathroom.

'Baby!' Aiden hissed as the door slammed shut.

Although Timothy didn't know it, his father had been waiting outside the bathroom and heard everything that had been said between the brothers. No sooner had Timothy stormed into his room, his father had collared Aiden in the bathroom.

'You shouldn't be so hard on your brother.' His dad had scorned. 'It isn't easy for him, you know.'

'I know.' Aiden had answered, eyes directed to the floor and unable to meet his father's stern gaze. 'Sorry.'

'Well, maybe in the morning you should make it up to him. Get to bed.'

Unaware of all of this, Timothy had paced the length of his room, still grumbling at what Aiden had said to him.

'He's just being mean.' Aleobe declared from somewhere in the room's corner.

'But he always does it,' Timothy complained. 'It's not like I want to have these dreams. He's not the only one who is fed up with them.'

'I know, son.' His dad answered, interrupting Aleobe just in time. 'That's why we are trying to help you as much as we can.'

'I know.'

'Right, it's late and you should be in bed.'

Timothy was about to explain what had happened in the bathroom, but thought better of it. The moment had passed and Aiden was now in his own room. Scrambling into his bed, he decided there would be no point in telling tales on his older brother and instead did his best to bury what Aiden had said as he rested his head on the pillow.

With the usual bedtime routines complete, his dad moved to the door and switched on the night-light plugged into the wall before turning out the main light. As the door closed, Timothy took a moment to scan and check all the dark corners of his bedroom. Satisfied there was nothing lurking in them, he rolled onto his side and clamped his eyes shut.

'I'm staying with you tonight.' Aleobe announced, his voice coming from the corner of Timothy's pillow. 'I hope we can keep it away for a night.'

'I hope so too.' Timothy muttered as he already felt sleep washing over him.

The pillow was soft and familiar. Before Timothy could even worry about the nightmares that lurked in the back of his head, he fell fast asleep.

***

The nightmare came, the same eyes burned and Timothy sat bolt upright in his bed.

'Tim I'm here.' Aleobe hushed from the end of the bed. 'It's OK, I'm here.'

Drenched in sweat, as was always the case afterwards, Timothy sat up in his bed and looked around the room wide-eyed. The terrifying image of the burning eyes haunted him, but there was nothing in the room but him.

'Was it the same dream again?'

'Yes.' Timothy answered as he wiped his brow with the back of his hand.

Perhaps it had been that deep down he knew Aleobe was in the room with him, but Timothy had not screamed as was normal when he tried to escape the nightmare. Sitting in the bedroom, part of him was disheartened by the fact his parents hadn't come running in. The other part was relieved that Aiden would not have more ammunition the following day.

Waiting for his body to stop quivering, Timothy soon felt the chill of the night. The layer of sweat on his skin chilled and he started to shiver in the bedclothes.

'You should get changed.' Aleobe offered.

'I want a drink.' Timothy replied as he swung his legs out of the bed and stood up.

Changing into fresh pyjamas, Timothy moved toward the door and pulled it open. A quick glance back at the clock beside his bed and was unsurprised it told the same time it always did:

03:10

Stepping into the hallway, Timothy felt very much alone on the wide landing. There was nothing to say anyone else was awake, and he felt very conscious of the silence.

Moving as quietly as he could across the carpeted landing and down the wooden stairs, Timothy made his way to the kitchen and poured himself a large glass of milk.

Sipping from the glass, he welcomed the cold milk, but there was something missing. Looking around the dark kitchen, the only light being from the open door of the fridge, he found the biscuit tin. Mustering all his stealth, Timothy prised the lid off and found the prize. Checking he was alone one last time, he took two biscuits and a third before he replaced the lid and moved to sit on a stool.

'It's nice in here.' Aleobe exclaimed from the centre of the island in the middle of the kitchen. 'I've not been in here much.'

'What do you like, Aleobe?'

'I look like me.' Aleobe laughed.

'Yeah, but I've never seen you.'

'What do you think I look like?'

'I have no idea.' Timothy confessed and downed the rest of the milk. 'I've never thought about it until now.'

'Would you like to see?'

Timothy chewed on the chocolate biscuit and pondered the offer. He had never thought about what his friend looked like, it had never been something he had thought about until that moment.

'How can I see you? I've never seen you before.'

'There is a way.' Aleobe started to explain, but a sudden noise silenced the both of them.

Somewhere upstairs, someone was out of bed. The creaking floorboards made Timothy's heart race. He stood from the stool and moved towards the door into the hallway.

Sneaking, making no more noise than a skulking midnight mouse, Timothy made his way to the bottom of the stairs as the bathroom light came on. Hiding from the beam of light, Timothy hid behind the banister and waited as his sister went to the toilet.

As he waited, a movement caught his attention and Timothy realised he was standing next to the old mirror. Bathed in the moonlight that poured through the glass of the front door, Timothy could see his pale reflection in the glass.

It hadn't been his movement that had caught his attention. It was something else. As he stepped closer to the mirror, he could see nothing but himself staring back. Upstairs, the toilet flushed, and he heard his sister washing her hands, but that didn't matter.

As the light in the bathroom went out, Timothy looked and watched Cathy sleep-walk back to her bedroom. When he was once again sure he was alone, Timothy returned his attention to the mirror, but something was wrong.

The reflection in the glass was wrong; there was something out of place about his reflection that appeared in the mirror. Where he had been looking up the stairs to Cathy but now stood facing the glass, his reflection was not doing the same.

In the mirror, he saw himself still looking up the stairs to where his sister had been.

Mouth agape, he watched as his reflection slowly turned to face him before it offered him a cheeky playful wink.

Timothy did the only thing that felt right. He ran up the stairs and jumped back into his bed.

CHAPTER FIVE

CURIOUS REACTION

MORNING ARRIVED FASTER THAN Timothy had expected. When he had jumped back into bed, still unnoticed by anyone else in the house, he had wrapped himself in the quilt like a protective cocoon. He was aware the feathers in the quilt would do little to protect him from anything, but it had made him feel better.

He had quickly become overheated under the covers and with a great deal of nervousness, Timothy had peeked out from beneath his shell to check the bedroom.

'No red eyes, no strange reflection, no monsters and no nightmares.' Timothy had whispered to himself.

With trepidation, Timothy had emerged from his shell like a curious tortoise. After holding the quilt high to his chin, just in case he needed to hide beneath it again, he had fallen back asleep.

Dreams came and went with no lasting effect and when Timothy was awoken by his younger sister, he was spritely and refreshed.

'Mum says it's time for breakfast.' Cathy beamed as she stood by his bed, her favourite teddy wedged under her arm.

'I'll be down in a minute.' He replied, his voice sounding groggy.

Cathy remained at his bedside, watching him. At eight, she was just on the cusp of being annoying, and while he found her amusing; she had some peculiar habits. Not appreciating other people's personal space was one of them. That morning was no exception.

'Give me some space, will you!' Timothy barked and his sister looked sad.

Her golden hair was messy and unkempt from having only just woken up. The bedraggled teddy bear beneath her arm had a sad expression that matched hers as her brother shouted at her. As the tears welled in her eyes, Timothy was awash with guilt straight away. Before he could say anything, she bolted from his room.

Laying his head back on the pillow, Timothy groaned as he knew what was coming next.

'Just for once,' his dad's voice carried up the stairs a few minutes later. 'Can't you three just be nice to one another?'

Sighing, Timothy climbed out of his bed and grabbed the dressing gown hanging off the back of his door. Ready for his inevitable telling off from his dad, he walked down the stairs as he tied the belt around his waist.

'What did you see last night?' Aleobe's voice sang as he reached the bottom of the stairs and the mirror.

'It was weird.' Timothy replied as he stepped off the final step onto the wooden floor of the hallway.

Moving with caution, he stepped across to stand in front of the mirror and for a moment closed his eyes in anticipation.

'What's wrong?' Aleobe pressed; although he couldn't feel him Timothy thought Aleobe was sat on his shoulder by the position of his musical voice.

'It was in the mirror last night.' Timothy whispered.

'The eyes?'

'I don't know, no, something different.'

'Open your eyes Tim.'

'I don't think I want to.' Timothy answered, his eyes remaining shut as he stood facing the mirror.

'Trust me.' Aleobe hushed and waited on his shoulder.

With reluctance, Timothy opened his eyes and looked at his reflection in the mirror. In the daylight, it felt somehow safer, less isolated and alone as the morning sunlight highlighted his flame-red hair in desperate need of a brush.

Much to Timothy's relief, the reflection was what it should be. The face looking back mirrored what he did and as he ran his fingers through his mop of hair, the figure in the mirror did the same.

'Last night it was different.' Timothy explained to Aleobe as he moved his way this way and that as if testing the reflection. 'When Cathy went to the toilet, I hid at the bottom of the stairs and waited. When I looked back at the mirror, it wasn't looking back.'

'I know.'

Aleobe's reply caught Timothy by surprise. There was something in his voice that told him his friend knew more than he was letting on.

'What do you mean?' Timothy asked.

'Last night we talked about something. Do you remember?'

'Seeing you, is that what you mean?'

'Yes.' Aleobe paused for a moment before continuing. 'You didn't give me a proper answer.'

Timothy pondered what his friend was asking.

'Yes.' He mumbled. 'I want to see you.'

'Then look.'

No sooner had Aleobe said the words did the reflection in the mirror shimmer. On his shoulder, in the place where he thought his friend would be, in the reflection he could now see Aleobe for the first time.

A few fingers larger than his hand, the only way Timothy could describe Aleobe was a winged miniature boy.

'You're a fairy.' Timothy gasped as he looked to his shoulder to find it empty. 'Where did you go?'

'I'm still here,' Aleobe giggled. 'And I'm no fairy!'

'Then what are you?' Timothy asked as he turned to look at the mirror and saw Aleobe sat on his shoulder still.

'I'm an Ecilop and please don't call me a fairy. These wings aren't just for decoration, like those little things you call fairies.'

Timothy watched as Aleobe strutted around on his shoulder, parading himself for Timothy to see in all his glory. Dressed in a pair of olive-green trousers, Aleobe's skin was a vibrant blue colour that seemed to shine in the bright morning light. Behind his pointed ears his emerald green hair sat down the centre of his back and was tied in a neat platted ponytail.

On the top of his head he wore a pair of curious looking goggles and his upper body was covered in a strange sleeveless top that looked to be in the pattern of scales.

What was most impressive about Aleobe, however, were his magnificent wings. In the sunlight, they shimmered a hue of purplish-blue, and the opaque wings glinted like gems as they fluttered behind him.

'What in an Eli-flop?'

'Ecilop!' Aleobe scorned as he waved a gloved finger at Timothy, joking. 'We are the guides for those who travel into my world. We are there to help them find their way.'

'And where do you come from?' Timothy pressed, his mind filled with wonder and curiosity.

'We call it Mielikuvitus and it isn't as far away as you'd think.'

'What does it look like?' A million questions raced through his head. 'What else is there? How many Eci-F... Ecilops are there? Who else lives there?'

'Slow down with the questions.' Aleobe chuckled as he jumped from Timothy's shoulder and somersaulted in the air in front of his face.

'But I want to know everything!'

'I have an idea,' Aleobe pondered as he floated in front of Timothy's face, still invisible save for the reflection in the mirror. 'Why don't I show you?'

'How?'

'Do you want to see?' Aleobe pressed. 'Are you sure you want to see?'

'Yes, yes more than anything.' An insatiable excitement bubbled in the pit of his stomach.

'Then look in the mirror.'

Aleobe turned to face the mirror, his excited face staring out through the glass at Timothy. Behind the flying Ecilop, Timothy once again noted his reflection. Just like the night before, it looked different from how it should. Where Timothy was standing with his arms by his side, the reflection raised its hand and waved at him.

Acting on instinct, Timothy returned the wave, noticing the fact he was using the opposite hand to the reflection, confusing his mind even more about what was happening. After the strange, yet cordial greeting, Timothy's reflection then reached forward and tapped its finger against the inside of the glass.

Overcome with nerves, Timothy felt encouraged by the broad smile on Aleobe's face. His once invisible friend had never steered him wrong and there was no reason not to trust him now.

'Touch the glass.' Aleobe encouraged in a whisper.

Raising his hand, Timothy extended his trembling finger and inched it towards the dusty glass of the mirror. As both his own reflection and the image of Aleobe smiled at him, he did not understand what he was doing. Doing his best to soothe the nervous shake in his hand, Timothy felt the tip of his finger touch the cold glass of the mirror at the point where his reflection had done the same.

In an instant, before he could change his mind, the hand on the other side of the glass reached out towards him and took hold of his wrist. Before a sound could escape his lips, it dragged Timothy from where he stood and pulled him into the mirror, leaving the hallway once again silent and empty.

CHAPTER SIX

MIELIKUVITUS

THE SOUND OF WATER was the first thing Timothy noticed. Even with his eyes closed, he could hear water tumbling over rocks and the sun made it bright behind his eyelids. Feeling his head spinning, Timothy stayed as he was and tried to work out what had just happened.

The mirror in the hallway. His reflection and the hand grabbing him.

The memory of the hand emerging from the glass sent a shiver of fear down his spine and he sat bolt upright, opening his eyes. The first thing he saw, as his eyes adjusted to the harsh sunlight, was Aleobe hovering in front of his face.

'Don't get up. Take a minute to sit still.'

Timothy took in Aleobe as his wings fluttered and his shimmering blue skin caught the light. It dawned on Timothy as he watched the flying Ecilop, his once invisible friend, was not a reflection and was physically in front of him.

Focused only on the fluttering wings, Timothy raised his hand and reached his hand out to touch Aleobe.

'I'm not a pet bird, you know.' Aleobe laughed as he performed a loop-the-loop over Timothy's extended hand. 'Hold your hand out then.'

Doing as he was told, Timothy turned his hand over and Aleobe landed on his palm. Although Aleobe was standing on his hand, Timothy couldn't feel any weight to the small Ecilop. With great care not to unbalance his friend, he moved his hand closer to his face until Aleobe was standing a short distance from the tip of his nose.

'That's a bit close!' Aleobe grinned as he sat cross-legged to look at Timothy.

'Sorry,' he moved his hand back a little. 'Is that better?'

'Sort of, but it's ok. I guess it's weird seeing me?'

'Just a little.' Timothy confessed, as he looked at Aleobe with curiosity. 'Where am I?'

'Mielikuvitus, my home.'

With his answer, Aleobe raised his arm and directed Timothy's attention to the world around them. As he moved his attention from Aleobe, Timothy realised he had been so focussed on his friend he had not taken in his surroundings.

What Timothy saw stunned him into silence.

A wild river roared in front of him as he sat in a glade of bright-green grass. A warm breeze wafted the tall blades of grass all around. The water crashed against a handful of jagged rocks that sat proud of the surface and on the far shore a line of trees moved in the breeze.

It was the leaves of the trees that stole his attention as they were a mixture of greens, pale blues and purple. Timothy had seen nothing so colourful and the colours of the leaves seemed impossible for his brain to process.

He was about to ask a question when a sudden movement caught his attention.

From between the trees, a shimmer of silver caught his eye and Timothy turned to look for the source. There was something moving beyond the tree line, but he could not make out what it was. As the creature passed behind one tree trunk, then the next, all he could make out was the creature's size.

The movement stopped without warning and Timothy scanned where he had last seen it to try and identify the source. Still holding Aleobe in his hand, he stood up and walked to the edge of the rolling river to see if he could see the movement again.

As he reached the banks of the river, he caught sight of movement again. Unlike before, the movement was between two thick trunks of the pastel-leaf trees as a brilliant-white stallion emerged from the woods.

The horse cantered towards the far bank of the river, and its mane of golden hair wafted as it moved. As Timothy took in the full grandeur and beauty of the animal, something peculiar caught his attention.

Standing proudly from the centre of the horse's head, above the line of its eyes was a twisted and pointed horn that shimmered as it moved.

'That's a... a...' Timothy stammered, struggling to form a sentence.

'A unicorn, yes.' Aleobe continued as he stood up and back-flipped off Timothy's hand.

Timothy could not believe what he was seeing. Suddenly, a unicorn foal emerged from the tree line to join the larger creature. In a matter of moments, from having been standing in the hallway of his family home, his reflection had dragged him through a mirror and now he was staring at a creature he had only ever believed existed in stories.

'How is this possible?'

'This is Mielikuvitus Timothy. This isn't your home, it's mine.' Aleobe fluttered out across the river and danced across the surface of the tumbling water.

Timothy watched as his friend dived beneath the surface of the water and disappeared for a second. A little further down the river, Aleobe exploded from beneath the surface of the water and flew fast and high into the sky. As he did, he left a trail of water behind that tumbled back to the river and all Timothy could see was the rainbow of colours within the droplets.

'This is Rainbow River,' Aleobe beamed as he spun in the air, sending droplets of colourful water spiralling in every direction. 'The water looks normal from the surface, but beneath it is every colour of the rainbow. In the sun, it looks like this!'

Aleobe was in his element as he introduced his best friend to his homeland. The little Ecilop danced in the air and skimmed the surface of the water as he corkscrewed the width of the river, scooping handfuls of the colourful water to throw as he moved.

Timothy was entranced by what he was saying. The erratic movement of Aleobe had caught the attention of the regal unicorn as it moved to protect its young from the crazed antics of the excited Ecilop.

'The river has been here since the first days of Mielikuvitus and legend has it that the water feeds into everything and gives us life.' Aleobe chattered in excitement as he tried his best to explain everything as fast as possible. 'My mother used to say that's why our skin is blue.'

Aleobe dived beneath the turbulent surface of the river once again and as Timothy waited for some spectacular explosion of colour, a new voice caught his attention.

'Excuse your friend there,' the new voice announced from behind him. 'He has been very excited about showing you this place since he very first arrived in your life.'

Timothy turned to identify the source of the voice, but all he saw was a grey border collie sat on the grass a short distance behind him. The dog's blue eyes stared at him as Timothy searched for the person who had spoken.

'I expect my natural appearance isn't something you would be used to,' the *dog* said and once again Timothy's mouth dropped open in shock. 'Allow me to present myself so you may feel more comfortable with me.'

The dog stood itself up and turned so Timothy could see its side profile. It's long grey, brown and white fur looked well-groomed and healthy. As the dog walked away Timothy watched as the dog transformed into a grown man.

'What the...' Timothy gasped.

'My name is Sky,' the man announced as he turned to face Timothy, who was rooted to the spot on the banks of the Rainbow River.

The man, Sky, looked to be in his early twenties, with a trimmed beard that matched the colours of the dog's fur. A medieval heavy cloak hung over his shoulders with the lining of fur, again matching that of his canine appearance, covering all the cloak's edges.

The oddest thing about Sky's appearance was his eyes. To Timothy, they looked odd, as they were the only part of him that had remained unchanged. Instead of human eyes, Sky's eyes remained as a dog's, the same piercing crystal-blue that remained fixed on Timothy.

Aleobe exploded through the surface of the river again and started to speak, but fell silent as Sky's attention turned to him.

'I would have expected at least a little warning you would bring your Ward.' Sky remarked, and Aleobe's joviality disappeared.

'I'm sorry,' Aleobe apologised as he flew back to Timothy's side and landed on his shoulder. 'It wasn't as I planned. I know I should have told you, I just thought...'

Sky silenced Aleobe with a raised hand and a warm smile.

'It's fine Aleobe, you know what's best for him.' Sky returned his attention to Timothy as he continued. 'Now Timothy, I think it is best we begin your exploration of Mielikuvitus in a more structured way.'

Sky held out his hand, and for a moment, Timothy hesitated.

'It's fine,' Aleobe whispered into his ear. 'Sky is someone you can trust here. He's lived here for centuries and I trust him.'

'How are you with Beaming?'

'Beaming?'

'Ah, yes.' Sky waited for Timothy to take his outstretched hand. 'You see those mountains in the distance?'

Timothy looked and saw a line of jagged mountains far away in the distance.

'Yes.'

'We are going there.'

'How?'

'Like this.'

With a loud crack of thunder, Timothy was ripped from where he stood and by the time his heart had taken a beat, he found himself stood at the base of the mountains he had seen.

CHAPTER SEVEN

HALO COVE

TIMOTHY GASPED IN SURPRISE as he yanked his hand free from Sky's soft grip. Staggering backwards, he felt as if someone had tossed him through the air with impossible speed. In the short time, less than a second, Timothy had felt air whipping past his face and the world around him had blurred all around him.

Releasing Sky's hand and moving away, he was astounded to find he was no longer stood on the banks of the Rainbow River. His surroundings were different from the grassy plains and rolling river as he now found himself stood on a raised platform looking out across a wide cove with sea and sand.

'Breathe!' Sky announced as Timothy started to feel light-headed.

As the world started to spin, Timothy staggered towards an ornamental wall that sat on the far side of the viewing platform. As his hands found stability with the warm stone, he tried to draw in a breath but couldn't. His throat felt tight. No matter how hard he tried, there was nothing he could do to draw breath into his screaming lungs.

'What's wrong with him?' Aleobe pleaded as he hovered in front of Timothy, his face painted with concern.

'His body is not used to the sudden movement.' Sky barked as he took hold of Timothy's shoulders and turned him around.

Timothy felt the panic rising as the world started to swim around him.

'Focus on me Timothy.' Sky instructed, but try as he might, Timothy could not fix his attention on Sky without his eyes wandering. 'Close your eyes and listen to my voice.'

Much against his fading senses, Timothy did as he was told. As the world went black, he focussed on Sky's calm voice and did everything he could to do what he said.

'Picture a flower in spring in your mind. See it opening in the crisp sun and as the petals open you will feel your body relax.'

Timothy tried fighting against the sleepiness that was growing inside him. Trying his hardest, he focussed his mind enough to picture a flower. Although the image was fogged and distant, Timothy could just about make out the budding red rose. It was the same as his mother grew in the greenhouse at home.

'As the flower opens, feel how refreshing that is, how relaxing it feels.'

Much to his surprise, Timothy felt his body relax until, without warning, his throat opened and the cool sea air rushed into his lungs. As the relief washed over him he opened his eyes and felt a sense of calm at the fact, he could breathe again.

'What was that?' he gasped between gulping in mouthfuls of air. 'What just happened to me and where am I?'

Sky took a step back, the fur edges of his cloak wafting just above the sandstone floor. He allowed Timothy a moment to regain his composure as he once again rested his weight on the pale stone balustrade.

'This is Partum City and what you see in front of you, out there,' Sky pointed out across the sea. 'Is Halo Cove.'

Timothy peered over the balcony edge and across a wide expanse of water. Starting with the golden sands of the beach far below, he traced the sand as it arched around to the far side of the sea. Between the white crests of the waves, he could just make out the far shore and to his left he saw where the land parted enough to allow access to the ocean beyond.

A solitary ship sailed between the jagged edges of the land, its pink mainsail slapping in the sea-breeze as the small ship bobbed its way across the cove.

'Halo Cove has been the capital of Mielikuvitus for longer than my life. We believe it was home to the first inhabitants of the land who arrived through that very passageway.'

Sky pointed out towards the narrow parting where the pink-sailed ship had just arrived.

'Who lives here?' Timothy asked as his sense returned to him and his mind flooded with questions.

'For many centuries, almost all inhabitants of the land,' Sky trailed off in a moment of thought. 'But now it is more a gathering place where some still live, but all creatures have found their own place in Mielikuvitus.'

'It's very grand.' Timothy remarked as he turned around to look at the city behind him.

The city itself appeared to have been grown from the living rock. There were no obvious joins in the structures that towered from the impressive mountainside. It stood taller than any mountain Timothy had ever seen. The summit, far above the clouds, was impossible to see and even though he craned his neck, there was no sign that the mountain ended at any point.

Around the ground, the rock had been carved into an array of structures. Unlike the cold grey stone of the mountain, the buildings looked to be made of brushed sandstone and quartz crystal.

Everything, as Timothy could see, was rounded and smooth. There were no obvious angles amongst the buildings and everything seemed to flow towards an intriguing feature that sat on the far end of the raised courtyard he now found himself stood on.

A long, shallow slope stretched up to a platform that was shrouded beneath a half-orb of opaque crystal. The sunlight that peeked through the lumbering clouds glinted off the smooth surface and, even from this distance, Timothy could make out a large table shielded from the elements by the orb.

Looking around, everything about the surrounding city flowed toward the angular platform and open ball of smoothed mineral.

'What's that?' Timothy pointed up at the raised altar. 'Up there.'

'That is the Table Of Haras and was once the seat of all power in Mielikuvitus.'

'Once?'

'When there was a need to organise ourselves in protection against dark forces.'

'But you don't need that anymore?'

Timothy had so many questions about the world he now found himself in. He could see Sky wanted to talk. There was, however, a hesitation from the young man in his answers.

'There wasn't,' Sky replied and did not give Timothy time to ask what he meant. 'There is a lot you need to understand and now is not the time.'

Timothy caught sight of a maroon-coated unicorn stood at the base of the slope leading up to the table. Sky's attention now seemed split between Timothy and the majestic creature as it stood at the base of the slope.

'I must take my leave and hand you to your friend, Aleobe.' The warm smile returned to Sky's face. 'I have matters to attend but would offer you an invitation to dine with me tonight.'

'Erm, yes.'

As Sky offered a nod of respect and dismissed himself, it dawned on Timothy how implausible and impossible all of what was happening could seem.

'Am I dreaming?' Timothy asked as he turned to look back towards Halo Cove.

Aleobe had ceased his flying and now sat perched on the edge wall looking out across the cove. The little Ecilop rocked his legs back and forth as he peered out across the view, deep in thought.

'You're not dreaming Timothy. This is all very real.'

'How can it be?' Timothy pressed as he rested himself on the stone beside his once invisible friend. 'This time yesterday you were just a voice that has spoken to me since I was a baby. Now I'm stood in some strange place seeing the most magical things and you expect me to believe it is all real?'

Without warning, Aleobe stamped his small foot on the tip of Timothy's finger, sending a jolt of pain through his hand.

'What did you do that for?' Timothy snapped as he pulled his stinging hand off the stone.

'Did you feel something?' Aleobe grinned, a mischievous look painted on his face.

'You know I did.' Timothy groaned as he inspected the end of his pointing finger, which now glowed red.

'Then you're not dreaming then are you?'

'I guess not!' Timothy groaned as he soothed his painful finger.

'How about I show you around and later you can ask more questions of Sky.'

Timothy wanted to know everything but realised it was not the time to bombard Aleobe, or Sky, with questions from a curious twelve-year-old's mind. Accepting the invitation, he placed his throbbing hand in his pocket and followed as Aleobe fluttered up to rest once again on his shoulder.

CHAPTER EIGHT

DINING WITH ROYALTY

S KY STOOD ON THE long gangway that stretched out over the golden sands of Halo Cove. The pink-sailed ship bobbed in the water a short distance from the dock and the cloaked man seemed deep in thought. As Timothy stepped closer, he felt a wave of unease at disturbing his host.

Aleobe had been more than excited to show Timothy the sights of the capital city. They had begun at the base of the long ascending slope to the Table Of Haras and while his friend had not taken him to the top; he had given Timothy a potted history of the Table.

Meandering the city streets, Aleobe had explained that there had once sat a council of skilled mystics known as Partum Spiritus. They had formed together with representatives of all inhabitants of Mielikuvitus and established themselves as guardians against dark forces.

Timothy had been hooked on Aleobe's every word. In his mind he could see every battle that the excitable Ecilop recounted to him.

'What happened to the Partum people?' He had asked as the stories trailed to an end.

'The Partum Spiritus, you mean?' Aleobe had corrected as they reached the edge of the city furthest from Halo Cove. 'When the threat of darkness was gone, and the age of peace reigned, they were no longer needed.'

'Where did they go?'

'When they were seated at the Table, they were powerful, but when their need was no longer there, they returned all power to those who lived here. With a promise to return if ever we needed them, they sailed from the shores in ships made of emerald and gold.'

'To go where?'

Timothy was hooked, drinking in the rich history that Aleobe offered him.

'Nobody knows, the last Partum left before I was born.'

Looking at the large perimeter wall that marked the edge of Partum City, Timothy noticed the fact someone had removed the gates and the wall sat open.

'Where are the gates?'

'When the Partum Spiritus left, there was no longer a need for defences. They left Mielikuvitus in a time of peace and they agreed it amongst the Elders that all aspects of the land would be open for free passage.'

As a herd of elephants stomped through the wide opening in the wall, Timothy felt the hovering Ecilop was holding something back. Timothy's mind had wandered as the elephants walked along the avenue leading into the city, guided only, it seemed, by their knowledge of the grand city's layout.

'Oh my, look at the time!' Aleobe had exclaimed, to Timothy's amusement.

'What time is it?' Timothy realised he had no watch and had seen no clocks on their journey through the city streets.

'Time we got you back and got you ready.'

'Ready?'

Aleobe had not given Timothy any time to ask questions as he guided him back toward the wedge of polished crystal and stone that dominated the skyline at the centre of the city. As they made their way back, Timothy was afforded the opportunity to see Partum City in all its glory. As the waning sun painted the city in a rich red colour, he passed handfuls of curious creatures along the way.

Where the sight of the golden-mane unicorn had caught his breath at the banks of the Rainbow River, it was nothing compared to the residents of Partum. On his tour of the city, Timothy had seen Ecilop of every skin colour, unicorns, human-sized ravens, centaurs and a handful of creatures he did not recognise and would struggle to even describe.

With no opportunity to ask questions, Timothy had followed Aleobe to a small building close to the shore of Halo Cove. At one particular dome-roofed building, an old woman clothed in an orange dress welcomed him at the open door.

'You must be Timothy,' the woman had greeted. 'I have heard a lot about you over the years. You are much bigger than I imagined.'

The woman looked incredibly old; her weathered and wrinkled skin giving away the centuries of her life. That said, however, her presence was warm and welcoming as she ushered Timothy through the low door into the room beyond.

Inside the domed building, Timothy was met by an army of flying creatures. Not too dissimilar to Aleobe, these were stumpy looking creatures with shorter wings and wider bodies. As they hovered around him, they started to take measurements and tug at his clothes, sizing him up as he moved deeper into the building.

'Is he to meet the Elders tonight?' The woman asked as she walked ahead of Timothy.

'Yes,' Aleobe beamed. 'He has already met Sky, but they have invited him to dine with the Elders.'

The old woman stopped and turned to look at Timothy.

Moving with surprising speed, the old woman stalked up to him and drew a large magnifying glass from the waistband of her dress. Inspecting Timothy's clothes, in fact his pyjamas he had kept on from waking in his room, he felt self-conscious about his appearance.

'You wear these clothes where you come from?' The old woman asked with a tut. 'Not the clothes of any respectable guest of the Elders.'

'I wear them to sleep in; we have other clothes to wear during the day.'

The old woman ignored Timothy's answer as she waved her hand in the air, sending the overweight fairies into a frenzy of activity.

'You will be presented appropriately. That is why you are here.'

The fairies zigzagged through the air this way and that as the old woman measured and adjusted her tape measure around various parts of Timothy's torso, arms and legs. At last, when she had measured every length and angle of his body, a line of hovering creatures held a variety of rich fabrics in their hands for her to inspect.

'Too cold, too warm, too regal, too red, too green, not red enough, too orange, too much, not enough.' The old woman moved along the line. Each time she dismissed the fabric, the fairy would fly away.

After circling the entire room, she settled on a black fabric with silver stitching.

'This will be the one.' She declared with pride and peered at the fabric through the magnifying glass. 'You should clean yourself up. By the time you have finished your clothes will be ready.'

The old woman pointed to a door on the far side of the room and, encouraged by Aleobe, Timothy had moved through into the small bathroom.

She had been right. By the time Timothy had cleaned himself and returned to the main room, he was in a state of shock to find four of the fairies waiting outside the door with a tailored two-piece garment held between them.

Timothy admired the clothes. Quite how the old woman and her helpers had made it in such a short space of time was beyond his comprehension. Having wandered the streets filled with impossible creatures, however, Timothy was happy to accept that almost anything was possible in Mielikuvitus.

'The trousers should fit you but can be adjusted inside with these buttons,' the old woman explained as Timothy took the trousers and slid them on.

The material was light and as he adjusted the waist, it almost felt like he was wearing nothing on his legs. Feeling the soft fabric against his skin, it felt warm to the touch and as he admired the intricate stitching and detailed pattern on the seams he was interrupted by more explanation of his new clothes.

'Your top is again adjustable to you, but there shouldn't be much need for that.' The old woman helped him slide the top of his head. 'And here is the side-cloak.'

'The what?'

'As a guest of the Elders, we expect you dress appropriately. This should be tied around your neck and hung over your right arm.'

The old woman tied the fine ribbon around his neck and adjusted the cloak, so it sat covering the whole of his right arm.

'Really?' Timothy scoffed. 'I feel like some over-dressed pirate.'

'Yes, really,' the old woman barked as she smoothed the cloak with her wrinkled hand. 'Sucatraps will not present you to the Elders dressed in bed-clothes!'

'That's her name, before you ask.' Aleobe hissed into his ear as the old woman neatened out a ruffle in the fabric.

'There!' She announced. 'Now you are ready.'

Feeling over-dressed, like he was going to a fancy-dress party, Timothy had been ushered out of the old woman's abode and guided out towards the gantry where Sky was waiting.

As he waited on the wooden dock, Timothy looked at the pink-sailed ship and wondered what his host was thinking. After what felt like an age Sky turned to face him and the look of concern painted on his face was replaced with a warm smile.

'I see you have been to see Sucatraps,' Sky nodded in approval as he walked to Timothy and admired his clothes. 'She has excelled herself.'

Toying with the cloak hanging from his right side, Sky looked down at Timothy.

'Are you ready to dine with royalty, Timothy?'

'Can Aleobe come?'

'It's not my place tonight,' Aleobe answered. 'This is your time; I will be here when you're done.'

For a moment, Timothy was unsure about leaving his friend, but he knew enough to respect what was being said.

'Who am I going to meet?' Timothy asked as Sky walked with him off the dock and back toward the houses on the edge of the city.

'The Elders, those who represent the creatures of Mielikuvitus.'

Sky and Timothy walked together in silence. As they passed between two carved statues of perching ravens, Timothy cast a glance back to Aleobe who sat on a wooden post at the edge of the dock.

Timothy felt a wave of nerves as he lost sight of his friend and felt uncertain about who, or what, he was about to meet.

CHAPTER NINE

FEASTING IN HONOUR

T HE WELCOME TIMOTHY RECEIVED was something he would never have expected. Passing through a large arch-way beneath the long slope leading to the Table Of Haras, Sky guided him into a vast chamber.

'You are the first of your kind to step foot in here for many years.' Sky explained as they walked across the wide open space.

Looking around, the grandeur of the room was astounding. Figures and statues had been carved into the face of the sur-rounding walls. They had covered the ceiling in a bright-painted fresco showing, Timothy assumed, key times in Mielikuvitus' history. In a bronze bowl suspended from the ceiling, a fire roared above a hexagonal table, illuminated the room.

There was more light, fed by various similar bronze bowls of burning fire held in the hands of robed stone statues around the room's edge. Although the flames danced in the warm air, the shadows seemed not to move and it filled the room with light and heat.

'I will make introductions in their true form first and then allow them, if they wish, to take an alternative appearance as I have.' Sky murmured as he guided Timothy towards the enormous table.

Gathered beyond the table was a sight that took Timothy a moment to comprehend. The maroon-coated unicorn caught his attention first as the regal creature turned its head to look at them as they approached.

'That is Nasser, honourable father of the unicorns you saw on the banks of Rainbow River.'

The tall unicorn lowered its head to the ground in greeting as Sky made his introduction. With the greeting done, the tall creature turned away from Timothy and the last thing he noticed, before the creature transformed into a human, was the shape of a star in golden hair on the hind of the great unicorn.

'I am pleased to make your acquaintance, Timothy Scott.' Nasser declared, his voice powerful. 'You are most welcome to our lands.'

'Thank you.' Timothy replied, feeling even more self-conscious at the welcome of the magnificent creature.

Like Sky, Nasser transformed from animal to human in front of Timothy. Nasser now stood as a middle-aged man adorned in a cloak of fine material the same colour his body had been as a unicorn. The horn that had sat proud from the centre of his head was still present but, much to Timothy's relief, it had shrunk in as Sky's had, Nasser's eyes remained the same when human as in his natural unicorn appearance. The deep brown colour and oblong pupil looked a little too large for his face, but the next introduction stole Timothy's attention.

'This is Etak the Raven Queen.'

Shifting his attention, Timothy gasped as an enormous jet-black raven flew onto the table in front of him. In the flickering light of the fire, the bird's oily feathers shimmered. Once again, the creature lowered its head before making its transformation into a human.

Unlike the transformations of Sky and Nasser, Etak flew into the air in a dramatic spiral and completed her metamorphosis mid-flight. As the young black-haired woman landed on the floor behind the table, she offered Timothy a wry smile.

Much the same as Nasser and Sky, Etak kept the black-eyes of her animal. Even though she had taken on a human appearance, her face had a pointed essence to it and as he took in her appearance, Timothy could see the resemblance to the raven she was.

She looked to be in her early twenties, but Timothy was learning not to put any stock or faith in appearances in Mieliku-vitus. Her black hair was short and cropped just above her neckline. What would have been her wings looked to be her own cloak draped with feathers covering her arms before wrapping around to the centre of her back. Timothy could not be sure, by looking at them, if it was a garment or, in fact, her very wings folded behind her. Her upper arms were now tattooed with intricate feathers in black-ink down to each elbow.

'Nasser and Etak come from the Brightlands and those creatures that dwell near the Mystic Forest.'

'Where is that?'

'My apologies,' Sky corrected. 'I forget myself and the fact you have seen so little of our lands. That will come in time and you will no doubt become familiar with all aspects of Mielikuvitus.'

'Nitram,' a stern voice declared from behind Nasser.

The creature that appeared next sent a curious shiver down Timothy's spine. Taking an involuntary step back Timothy took in the strange appearance of what, for all intents and purposes, was a fish with legs and feet.

'May I present Nitram of the Hegel-Steffi and the Waterlands?'

The fish-man bore the appearance of a bulbous clownfish and looked awkward as he moved toward the table and rested his oversized fins on the edge to stare at Timothy. Unlike the others he had been introduced to there was something less welcoming about Nitram. As the fish offered a curt nod, nothing as respectful as Etak or Nasser, the leg-feet-fish, as Timothy named it in his head, blinked its bulbous eyes.

'You will forgive me for remaining as I am,' Nitram gargled, his voice sounding like it was still underwater. 'The presence of legs when I encroach on the land is enough for me.'

'Whatever suits you best.' Sky hid his disappointment well, so well that Timothy missed the scowl his host threw at the defiant fish.

'So,' Sky began and waved for everyone to move to the table. 'We have representatives of the Brightlands, the skies, the water and...'

The sound of a door opening behind them caught Timothy's attention, and he turned to see who had arrived. As she stepped into the light of the burning fire, Timothy recognised Sucatraps as she walked slowly towards them.

The old woman was no longer dressed in the tattered orange gown but now in an ethnic dress that floated along the ground behind her in a short train. Unlike in the small dome-roofed abode, she was now supporting her weight on a crooked cane of stained wood.

'We have the representative of the Free People.' Sucatraps announced in her soft voice. 'My apologies for the lateness of my arrival, but my last customer presented somewhat of a challenge in the design of their garments.'

Timothy felt the eyes of the others focus on him and his cheeks reddened in response. Smoothing the fabric to ease his nerves, Timothy watched as the old woman threw him a cheeky grin.

'I'm joking, young Timothy,' she soothed. 'I am late because I choose to be, nothing like keeping the all-powerful Elders waiting a little longer than they think they need to.'

Timothy was seeing an almost childish cheekiness in the old woman. As she held out her arm, he took it and she guided him to the table. As they reached the seats Sucatraps tugged on his arm to draw him closer so she could whisper in his ear.

'While I can excuse the fact, you are not used to the clothes,' she rubbed her hand over Timothy's uncontrollable hair. 'I would have expected you to have done something about your hair.'

Allowing the old woman to tame the mess of red hair, Timothy once again blushed as Sky chuckled, taking his seat beside him.

'She's like that with all of us.' Sky chuckled. 'It's the price we pay for her unique tailoring.'

'Oh, sit down and quiet your tongue. Remember who is the oldest of us here now.'

Feigning a look of embarrassment, Sky threw Sucatraps a knowing smile and turned to address the rest of the table.

'My honoured guests, we have gathered here to welcome Timothy Scott to Mielikuvitus.' Timothy's cheeks remained bright red. 'Might I suggest it is time for us to eat?'

Without waiting for an answer, Sky slapped his palm onto the surface of the table and it plunged the room into darkness.

Unable to see anything, Timothy was grateful to feel Sucatraps' wrinkled hand rest on his leg as sensed him tensing in the dark. With no visible light, Timothy struggled to make out anything until, after a few seconds of eerie silence, Sky repeated the sound of his hand hitting the table.

As the sound echoed around the room, the burning fires flickered back to life. Those around the edge of the room were first, bathing the far edges of the room in light until the large bronze bowl suspended above the table coughed to life. At first there was nothing more than embers, but very soon the sparks flew and in a *whoosh* of light the flames returned and the fire roared above them.

As it had transfixed his attention on the bowl of fire, Timothy had not noticed the table was no longer empty. Dropping his gaze to the table, he gasped as the whole surface of the hexagonal table was covered in foods of every type, some of which Timothy did not recognise.

In front of him, a silver chalice bubbled as a mist drifted from its lip over the surface of the table.

'It is customary for the guest to raise a toast but you are not accustomed to our rituals, so I offer my services.'

'Erm, ok then.' Timothy stammered.

'To the gathered Elders I raise a toast to you all and welcome the changing winds that will once again see Mielikuvitus prosper in peace and serenity.'

Timothy watched as Sky lifted his own cup from the table and took a long drink from the bubbling, misting liquid held inside it. Filled with nervousness, Timothy looked to his own chalice and lifted it from the table toward his face.

'You'll like it, I promise.' Sucatraps beamed as she gulped from her own drink. 'It tastes just how you imagine.'

'I don't know what I imagine.' Timothy replied as he sniffed the contents but could smell nothing.

Not wanting to offend his guests, Timothy placed the cold cup to his lips and tasted the chilled contents.

No sooner had it touched his tongue did Timothy gulp down the contents. It tasted perfect, better than perfect in fact, as his taste buds registered almost every enjoyable flavour he had tasted in his life.

'That, my boy, is Nectar and is very much a delicacy of Mielikuvitus.'

'It's amazing!' Timothy gasped as he finished the contents, only to see the liquid refill itself as he placed the cup back on the table.

'How?'

Once again filled with wonder, Timothy watched as his hosts set about filling their plates with food. For the first time, he realised how hungry he was and joined them in eating.

CHAPTER TEN

PARTUM SPIRITUS

AFTER THEY HAD EATEN less than half the food dishes on the table, Timothy was stuffed. Dropping his hands to his stomach it surprised him how full he was. Everything he had recognised on the table, and some he hadn't, had passed his lips until he could eat no more.

Conversation flowed around him. Mostly Timothy listened to the chattering Elders gathered around. Discussions ranged from trade, farming, celebrations and all matters of stately business. Although he was overflowing with curiosity and questions, Timothy thought it best to sit, listen and keep conversation between himself and the Elders sat either side of him.

As they ate, he spoke with Sky and Sucatraps but felt the Nitram's eyes boring into him from the far side of the table. The fishlike creature had taken a dislike to Timothy that was obvious. The feeling was not lost on the young man as he ate his food, ever conscious of the bulbous eyes staring at him.

'I have a question.' Timothy huffed as he sat back in his chair and exhaled.

'What would that be?' Nitram snapped.

'Well,' Timothy stammered, caught by surprise the fish had been listening. 'I know Aleobe is from this place. Why isn't he here or one of his kind at the table?'

An uncomfortable silence descended on the gathering, and Timothy could feel everyone's gaze focussed on him. For a few long moments nobody spoke or offered him an answer and straight away Timothy knew he had overstepped.

'Sorry, I didn't mean to...' Timothy tried to recover but fell silent as Sky coughed.

All attention at the table turned to Sky, who rose with purpose from his seat.

'If I have the Elders' permission, I shall advance the proceedings?'

Hushed chatter erupted between the other Elders around the table for a moment.

'You may be excused with your guest.' Nasser answered on behalf of the others and Sky nodded in gratitude.

'Timothy?' Sky offered him the opportunity to leave the table.

Grateful of the invitation, the sudden silence having sent him into a sea of worried self-consciousness, Timothy stood from his seat. Timothy was used to that feeling of self-worry. It had been something that had plagued him for most of his life.

That moment when, for a split second, Timothy knew he had said something he shouldn't and his brain went off on a million tangents. Every thought of what others were thinking.

Trying to understand the glares or sideways glances and before long, Timothy wanted nothing more than to hide away from everyone.

That same familiar feeling of being overwhelmed had boiled inside him the moment the words had left his lips. Although he didn't say, he was grateful when Sky offered him the chance to leave the table. Fighting the urge to stand and run, Timothy moved as calm as he could following Sky out of the room.

'Sorry about that.' Timothy murmured as Sky guided him to a narrow door on the opposite side of the large room.

'About what?' Sky grinned. 'Asking a question, being curious or the fact that Nitram looked like he wanted to eat you?'

'The first, well, all of it.'

'You have nothing to apologise for Timothy, if you have a question, I'd rather you ask it.'

'Ok.'

'Oh, and as for Nitram the last time I saw him smile, he laid a dozen eggs on the floor of the hall, so you've done nothing wrong there.'

Unable to hide the relief, Timothy laughed as they moved out of the hall and into a narrow corridor.

'Where are we going?' Timothy asked as he cleared his throat to stop laughing.

'You'll see,' Sky answered with a wry grin.

Moving along the corridor, they soon found themselves at the bottom of a spiral staircase leading upwards. As Sky started his ascent of the stairs, Timothy followed close behind and soon felt his lungs protesting at the effort of the long climb up.

After what felt like an age of climbing the twisting staircase, they reached a landing and Sky stopped. As Timothy caught his breath, he saw they were standing in front of a grand wooden door. An impressive fresco had been etched into the wood. Struggling to breathe, Timothy scanned the images on the door, but Sky was not waiting for him to absorb all the detail.

'Beyond this door is the Table Of Haras. What you are about to be told has not been uttered outside the hall below.' Sky's voice was now sombre; the seriousness of his tone was not lost on Timothy. 'Do I have your trust?'

Timothy nodded.

'Do I have your confidence?' Sky pressed again.

'Yes.'

'Then the door is yours to open.' Sky announced, and stepped aside.

Timothy stared at the door as he stepped up to it and placed his hand against the smooth wood. Pushing the door, it surprised him how light it was and how it moved aside at his touch. As the door opened, it allowed him his first view of the black-marble table he had only seen from a distance at the bottom of the long slope.

Much to his surprise, the half-orb of opaque crystal painted the world in a bright, shimmering light as if he was underwater. Although the sky was dark with night, and a blanket of stars shimmered in the sky, it was the light of the moon that the crystal orb enhanced. The entire world in front of him was hypnotising and enchanting.

'You are the first in almost twenty of your years to step foot here.'

Timothy's attention dropped to the magnificent marble table where, to his surprise, Sucatraps was standing once again dressed in another different dress. Unlike the one she had worn for the grand meal, she was now adorned in a metallic blue dress with a heavy hood folded down her back.

'What, there have been no other humans here in that long?'

'No,' Sky interrupted. 'You are stepping here not as a child of your realm but as the Partum Spiritus you are.'

Timothy's brow furrowed as the words sank in. So far, they had fed him crumbs of what the Partum Spiritus were. From what he had learned, it was not something he believed he was. Aleobe had described them as protectors, powerful people who sat with the Elders in times of danger and conflict to help protect the lands of Mielikuvitus.

'I don't think...' Timothy stuttered.

'Join me here,' Sucatraps instructed, carefully interrupting Timothy's protests.

Swimming with confusion, Timothy moved to the marble table as Sky walked in silence behind him. Reaching the table, he saw an ornate box sat in the middle of the table. Looking from the box, he saw Sucatraps waiting for him to join her.

'I should first apologise that tonight has been one of grandeur and distraction.' Sucatraps began.

'What do you mean?'

'We brought you here for a reason Timothy, not the chance encounter that Aleobe had you believe.' The mention of his friend brought a new feeling of confusion. 'Your friend was tasked with protecting you as a child and guiding you here if we ever needed you.'

'And you are needed.' Sky added.

The world felt overwhelming. The all-too-familiar feeling of everything closing in on him grew and Timothy needed to escape.

'I need to go.' Timothy announced and backed away from the table.

'Timothy, you need to listen to what we have to say.'

'I need to go.' He repeated.

'Please.' Sky moved to block Timothy's hasty back step. 'Listen to what we have to say and then make your choice. I know this won't make sense, but you need to hear everything.

'I'm twelve-years-old,' Timothy snapped in frustration. 'You can't even think I'm here for something like that. You've got me confused.'

'Timothy Scott, son of Gerard and Susan Scott, brother of Aiden and Catherine, second-born.' Sucatraps' recount of his family and lineage stunned him. 'We have followed you since birth, as with your siblings. We are not mistaken that you are Partum Spiritus.'

'I can't be.'

'Listen to what we have to say and then you can make your own decision.'

Torn, stuck between the undeniable urge to run and the flicker of curiosity that burned inside him, Timothy faltered for a moment.

'Ok.' He sighed and turned back to face the black-marble Table Of Haras. 'I'll listen.'

Chapter Eleven

Fight Or Flight

T imothy struggled to concentrate at first. The warm welcome and joyful tour around Partum City now had a bitter aftertaste. As he stood at the side of the marble table, what hurt the most was the fact Aleobe had been part of it. The one person he had trusted for as long as he could remember had brought him this far on a lie.

He had always struggled to bring himself to trust people and now the hurt he always feared was all too real.

'I am sorry for the deception, but it was necessary.' Sucatraps began.

Every inch the adolescent Timothy fought against the desire to snap at Sucatraps in anger and frustration.

'It was necessary so we could show you Mielikuvitus without a tainted view of servitude and protection. I wanted you to see our world in all its glory.' Sky continued.

'Had we told you the reason for your passage through the mirror, it would not appear as it does to you now.'

Timothy listened, biting his tongue against the angry backlash he longed to unleash. Resting himself against the edge of the cold-stone table, he allowed his hosts to explain the reasons for their deception.

It was Sucatraps who started the explanation. She started by filling in the gaps that Aleobe had left in the potted history he had given Timothy. Sucatraps explained the nature of the Partum Spiritus and their place, aligned with the Elders.

'In a time of conflict, we needed protection and support from the lands beyond our shores. It was a time where the dark beings of the Shadowlands had grown in power and threatened the peace and serenity of Mielikuvitus.'

'The Shadowlands,' Sky interrupted. 'Are a place where disorder reigns and darkness grows. For years, we battled with the darkness in the Great War of the Torn Mountains. When we fought without the Partum Spiritus, it was almost certain that we could not hold the darkness back.'

'Mielikuvitus is a place of peace, one where war was once a concept we had banished from thought or consideration.' Sucatraps explained, her words tarnished with sadness. 'When the darkness grew, it spread like a disease, a dark growth that infected the purity of everything. The skies turned black, it tarnished the earth, and the disease started to spread.'

'When the Great War raged at its fiercest, we were lost. As a people, we were divided and accepted defeat until one walked among us.' Sky slammed his hand onto the table and the surface of the table became filled with a dense mist.

Timothy watched in a state of shock as the mist on the table took form and grew until it represented a map of Mielikuvitus.

'You'll see Halo Cove and the churning waters of Rainbow River.' Sky explained as he pointed out the features. 'Here stand the Torn Mountains, their jagged rocks are nature's defence and split the Shadowlands from the Brightlands.'

The impressive smoke map changed until the range of mountains stretched the length of the table. Once again, as the view changed, Timothy felt himself drawn to what appeared to be happening atop the plateau summit of the centre most mountain.

Scores of figures battled on the flat summit. Featureless manifestations of smoke they fought in a frenzied battle split between lighter and darker creatures. The image changed, zooming in to bring the battle to life and fill the table in front of him.

'Our Great War raged for nineteen cycles of day until it seemed all hope was lost.'

Darker figures took ground and soon, what remained of the lighter figures were penned against the steep edge of the plateau.

'When defeat was certain, an Ecilop, not too dissimilar from your Aleobe, screamed to the skies for help in our darkest hour.'

A speck of smoke spiralled into the sky and disappeared. As it did, however, something else appeared in the space between the light and dark figures of smoke.

Three figures emerged from the ground and stood as a barrier between the warring sides.

'All have died who saw the first arrival of the Partum Spiritus, but their legacy remains all the same. They say it was with a crash of thunder three figures emerged from the ground. Their backs to the Brightlands and faces towards the dark creatures of the Shadowlands.'

Timothy, entranced by the magical display in front of him, watched as the three figures stepped forward and engaged the dark creatures in battle. Whereas they moved as three independent things, it was obvious their intent was aligned. The weapons they wielded were curious, and as they fought, Timothy could see tendrils of fire burning from the hands of the Partum Spiritus figures.

'With weapons of fire and flame, they pushed back the creatures of the Shadowlands and banished them back to where they came from. With the Great War of the Torn Mountains ended, we thought we were done.'

'What happened? Did they come back?' Timothy longed to know more, his boyish curiosity once again taking hold.

'Without a doubt they would and the Partum Spiritus then turned to us. With their help, guidance and knowledge, we prepared and readied ourselves to return to face the darkness with a hope of banishing it for eternity.'

The smoke changed once again and showed the Table Of Haras and gathered beings from across the land in conversation with the three Partum Spiritus.

'With their guidance, we would learn to defend ourselves and, guided by them, we returned to the Shadowlands and banished the last tendrils of evil back into its source.'

'Because it was the Ecilop who somehow summoned the help of the Partum Spiritus, it became the tradition that each would have an Ecilop to guide them through their time in Mielikuvitus. A task passed along their generations and the thing that ties Aleobe to you.' Sky allowed the words to sink in.

As the mist covering the table evaporated, Timothy once again noticed the intricately designed box sat in the table's centre. He suspected it was no coincidence that the box had sat beneath the mountain plateau. The fading mist allowed his attention to fall to the box.

'On the day of your birth, Aleobe was given to you, to be your protector and guide. Should a need ever arise for the Partum Spiritus to return to Mielikuvitus, he would guide you here, to the Table and the Elders.'

'I am not one of them,' Timothy answered. 'I am just a boy, a *boy*.'

'Then why are you here?' Sucatraps bit. 'How is it you passed through the void and into our world if you were not born to help us in our time of need?'

'What need?'

'The darkness has returned.' Sky answered, his voice solemn. 'Whispers have grown of a Dark Entity, twisted and infected by shadow and darkness that seeks to retake Mielikuvitus and spread beyond our shores.'

'I'm not what you think I am.' Timothy pleaded as Sucatraps reached for the box on the table.

'You are who and what you do not think you are.' She unlatched the lip and turned the box to face Timothy. 'We have watched you since you were born. Seen you plagued by your ties to our world and be haunted by things you believed were not real.'

'The nightmares?'

'They are not nightmares Timothy,' Sucatraps hushed. 'They are visions of a world you did not, until now, know of.'

Timothy was about to answer, but his attention was on the box as Sucatraps lifted the lid. Resting on a cushioned interior sat a curious artefact, something he had never seen before. What looked to be a handle of wood and carved bone sat proudly on the material. It sat as long as his forearm and the curious item stole his complete attention.

'This is the weapon of the Partum Spiritus. It allows them to wield the flames.'

'Take it.' Sky encouraged but Timothy was defiant.

'We will teach you to harness your strength and power, but you must try.' Sucatraps tried her best to sound calm. 'Only with our help will you face it.'

'Face what?' Timothy snapped, fear coursing through his veins as the memory of the glowing eyes from his nightmare filled his mind.

'The Dark Entity, the visions you see in your dreams.'

'No!'

It was too much. Timothy could not escape the feeling of dread and fear that consumed him. He retreated away from the table wide-eyed and backed away from Sucatraps and Sky.

'Let me go, I want to go.' Tears streamed down his face as panic took hold. 'Send me home. Let me go home.'

From nowhere, Aleobe appeared and placed his tiny hand on Timothy's cheek. As soon as his blue skin touched his face, Timothy was transported back.

The Table Of Haras and impressive crystal orb disappeared with a flash of lightning and once again Timothy found himself stood in the hallway of his home at the bottom of the stairs. Panting, he looked around in a frenzy as he tried to understand what had happened.

'Come on Tim, your toast will be cold!' His mum announced, snatching him back from his confusion.

As he turned to look at her, she saw his tears and moved to hug him.

'What's wrong? What's Aiden said?' His mum asked as she hugged him close and started to call his brother to them.

'No, it wasn't him.' Timothy sobbed. 'It was just...'

'The dream?'

'Yes, it was that again.' He lied.

Held close to his mother's chest he glanced a peek at the ornate mirror mounted to the wall and felt his heart sink as he saw Aleobe's reflection in the mirror looking at him, the sadness clear on his small face.

Chapter Twelve

Back To School

T HE MORNING MOVED IN a haze and before Timothy realised; he was sat in his classroom at school. He moved through the morning of lessons before his attention returned and he recognised where he was. Having done everything on autopilot Timothy struggled to remember his first lessons and even the journey to school.

For the first time in as long as he could remember, Timothy felt alone. Since seeing Aleobe in the scratched glass of the mirror in the hallway his friend had not spoken to him. Having left Mielikuvitus in such haste he feared it had done something to his connection with Aleobe.

'Oh look,' a voice barked from across the corridor as Timothy moved between his last class and the dining hall.

Timothy knew the voice and his heart sank. Looking around, he made a quick dash to the side of the corridor and did his best to move into the small woodwork store room, without being seen. As he moved behind the door, he heard the voice again over the chatter of other students.

Doing his best to press himself into the shadow of the store room panic raced through him. Ever since starting secondary school that voice had plagued him. From the very first moment, when Timothy had been caught doodling in his textbook, the bully had latched onto him as a vulnerable target. Even though Aiden had tried to intervene it had done nothing other than make sure their interactions took place away from his older brother's protection.

Timothy had always been the outcast. He had very few people he would call friends but nobody he would spend constant time with. He did and always had, preferred his own company. It was in an English lesson in the first week when the over-activeness of his imagination had caught the attention of his peers.

'In here.' A voice boomed outside the door, and Timothy held his breath.

It was no use, if they had seen him come into the storeroom there was no escape and they would pin him in the room. The door rattled and in a flash a familiar face peered around the door with an evil grin.

'Look what we have here.'

Danielle Collier was a brutish-looking girl. Her thick-set features were framed with a round face and an upturned piggish nose. Timothy had always thought she was the perfect representation of a school bully. Even Aiden had commented on her picture-perfect appearance when Timothy had confided in him when he had first arrived at school.

'Trying to hide from me, Crazy Boy?' Danielle smirked.

The rotund schoolgirl was joined by another boy from her class whose name Timothy had never found out. Danielle only ever referred to him as Froggy, and he always answered to that. Froggy, another apt name, matched his bulging eyes and pale skin.

'Just leave me alone.' Timothy sighed and moved to push past Danielle.

As he made the move, he felt her heavy hand slam into his shoulder and propel him back into the corner. The air was knocked from him as his back slammed into the wooden shelving and the overweight bully was on him in an instant.

'Shut the door, Froggy,' Danielle growled. 'I don't want a teacher disturbing us this time.'

Obediently, her pale co-bully checked the corridor and closed the door, leaving them isolated from the crowds of school-children in the corridor. With the door secured, the dark room was bathed in the pale automatic light in the ceiling.

'Can't you just leave me alone?' Timothy barked as he massaged his back where it had hit the shelving on the wall.

'Why would I want to do that Crazy Boy?' She towered over him and pressed him into the corner. 'You're the boy that walks on his own, draws pictures and makes up stories. Nobody likes you.'

'I don't need them to!' Timothy bit back.

'Well, having a friend would be pretty helpful right now, wouldn't it?'

'Loner.' Froggy chirped with glee from behind Danielle.

'I can look after myself.' Timothy argued, and although it was a lie, he did his best to look confident.

As soon as the words had left his lips, he regretted it. Danielle's face went bright red in response to his defiance and she pressed her face to his, so close he could feel her breath on his face. Bearing down over him, she stared into his eyes with pure distaste and venom.

'Getting brave, are you?' She snarled as she buried a clenched fist into his stomach.

A chorus of cackling laughter surrounded Timothy as he doubled over from the power of the blow. He did all he could to hold back the tears welling in his eyes.

Not letting up, she grabbed his tie and lifted him to his feet until they were nose-to-nose.

'You'll do well to remember that nobody will miss you if you disappear. Nobody misses the freaks.'

So many answers flooded Timothy's head, but he couldn't pull himself to offer her a retort. Shrinking from her gaze, he dropped his eyes to the floor and felt the sting of her hand as she slapped him around the face and released her grip on his tie.

Dropping to the floor, the laughter resumed and with nothing more to offer, the pair of bullies disappeared back into the flow of lunchtime pupils, leaving Timothy alone in the storeroom.

Timothy stayed there for the rest of the lunch break and only emerged as the lunchtime bell echoed along the corridor outside.

Having pushed the door too with his foot, he had remained unseen, but even if the door had been open, he doubted anyone would have seen him.

Danielle Collier's words hurt all the more because Timothy knew them to be true. Having endured the first year of secondary school, he had always been the shadow on the fringes, content with his own company. Most of the time that went unnoticed and he could spend his time in the library writing stories or else researching something that had caught his attention that day.

As the world moved on without him, he felt aware of how unimportant he was to the world around him. Nobody cared where he was, nobody searched for him or even missed him in the lunch hall. That realisation itself hurt more today than it had done before.

It hurt because he was alone. Even Aleobe had abandoned him.

Gathering his belongings and blending into the crowds, Timothy endured the rest of the school day without incident and was relieved to get home and find the house empty. He knew his parents would be a little longer collecting Cathy from school and, at least for a short while, he had the house to himself.

Closing the stained-glass front door, he hung his bag on the peg, took off his shoes and walked along the hallway towards the living room.

As Timothy reached the mirror, he stopped.

The cracked glass in the bottom corner caught his eye as the sunlight reflected off the spider-web in the glass.

With a feeling of nervousness, Timothy turned to look at the mirror and saw his own dishevelled reflection looking back at him.

'Where are you?' He asked the mirror, hoping to see Aleobe in the reflection. 'I need a friend.'

There was no answer from the mirror as it reflected no movement other than the ones he made, much as it should be in the glass. Matching the feeling when he had left the storeroom after his interaction with Danielle, Timothy felt very much alone.

All but dragging himself up the stairs, Timothy stopped as he heard the sounds of movement in the study room and stopped dead on the landing. Leaning close to the door, he heard the rustling sound again and inched closer to the door.

As his hand reached for the handle, someone yanked the door open from the inside, making Timothy jump back. Heart racing, he tried to make sense of what he was seeing.

'What are you playing at?' Aiden scorned and Timothy had never been so relieved to see his older brother. 'Sneaking around like that, you idiot, almost gave me a heart attack.'

'Sorry,' Timothy apologised and moved to continue to his bedroom and think.

'What's up, little bro?' Aiden's voice changed.

'Nothing.' His answer came too quick and straight away Aiden sensed his younger brother was lying.

'Come on, I know you well enough. What's happened?'

Timothy avoided eye-contact with Aiden, instead focussing on a patch of flaking paint on the wall next to the bedroom door.

'Is it that Collier girl again?'

'No.' Timothy defended, but felt his cheeks flush with the lie. 'It's nothing; I just want to be on my own.'

Timothy moved to carry on to his bedroom, but Aiden grabbed his arm and turned him to face him. Tears filled Timothy's eyes, and he fought to stop them from falling down his cheeks.

'If it is her, then she's having it tomorrow.'

'I don't want more trouble.'

'Right, so it was.' Aiden growled. 'Nobody but me gets to pick on my little brother!'

The sudden kindness from his older brother relieved some feeling of loneliness and he could not help but allow the corners of his mouth to turn into a slight smile.

'Get yourself sorted, mum and dad will be back soon and I promise I'll sort Danielle Collier out in the morning.'

Timothy wiped the tears from his eyes and thanked his brother with a nod and a smile.

'Oh, by the way,' Aiden interrupted as Timothy reached his bedroom door. 'There was a weird box outside your door, so I put it on your bed.'

Timothy did not know what his brother was talking about and as he pushed the door open, his mouth dropped open as he saw the box Aiden was talking about.

There, sat on his bed, was the box Sucatraps had presented to him on the Table Of Haras. Just how the box was outside his room was a mystery and Timothy closed the door so Aiden would not grow too interested in the curious box.

CHAPTER THIRTEEN

INSIDE THE BOX

ALONE IN HIS ROOM Timothy stared at the box sitting proud on his bed. The shell of the box was cold to the touch and as he admired the craftsmanship of it he lifted the latch securing the lid in place. Although he knew what should be underneath, his heart increased its pace as he lifted the lid open.

The same crumpled blue material filled the box and sat in the middle of it was the same curious artefact Sucatraps had shown him.

'How is this possible?' Timothy muttered to himself as he sat on the bed staring at the curious item.

Tucked into the fabric on the underside of the lid Timothy noticed a folded piece of parchment and pulled it from its place.

Unfolding the sheet he found a note with a single word written in large artful letters, it read:

NOSYM

'Nosym,' Timothy read aloud. 'What does that even mean?'

'It's what that is called.' Aleobe's voice startled him and he looked around for his friend.

'Aleobe, where are you?'

'Right here. I've been waiting for you.'

Timothy watched as the blue fabric moved as Aleobe, remaining unseen, walked over the box. When the material stopped moving, Timothy guessed his friend had perched himself on the lip of the box.

'I had to bring this to you. Sky said it would help you realise where you belong and how much we need you.'

'It's not been a day for making me think I'm a hero.' Timothy replied, defeated.

'Those bullies again?'

'Yes.'

'Ignore them; I've watched you since you were a baby. I know what you are capable of.' Timothy shook his head as Aleobe spoke. 'If Sky, Sucatraps and the Elders believe you can become a Partum Spiritus, then I believe you can.'

'That's nice, but you're biased. After all, you're my,' Timothy paused for a moment before finishing his sentence. 'You're my *only* friend.'

'That's why I know you should come back to Mielikuvitus and become what we all believe you are.'

Timothy pondered the thought for a moment. Staring at the box and where he imagined Aleobe to be sitting, he could not help but allow his mind to wander. Even the slightest of possibilities that he could learn to be something more than the quiet boy haunted by nightmares and imagined things made the offer even more tempting.

'So what is it?' Timothy declared. 'This Nosym thing. What does it do?'

'In the right hands, it does everything.' Aleobe answered, full of glee. 'In the wrong hands, it does nothing.'

Timothy looked closer at the Nosym and took in its intricate detail. What had first looked like carved pale bone was, in fact, the same crystal they had constructed the buildings in Partum City from. Unlike the buildings, however, the crystal was milky, giving it the look of bone.

The wooden part in the middle was wrapped with leather and they had crafted finger-grooves into the wood to allow the Nosym to be held. As it was the lengths of his forearm, Timothy counted the grooves and realised it could be wielded in one or both hands.

The carved crystal at either end drew his attention the most. Someone had carved one end into the shape of a lion with is mouth wide as if trapped in a permanent roar. The opposite end was the head of a serpent, again its mouth open wide. Moving to peer into the lion's mouth, Timothy was surprised how dark it appeared and how impossible it was to see anything within the wood behind the carved crystal head.

'Pick it up.' Aleobe urged, but Timothy remained steadfast, his hands secure in his lap. 'It's yours.'

'It can't be mine. I've never seen it before and it's only mine because you've given it to me.'

'Wrong.' Aleobe chirped. 'Nosym was made for you the day you were born. Crafted by a Partum Spiritus to celebrate your birth.'

'Not possible.'

'Last night you would have said that about Mielikuvitus and now look at you. You've crossed into another world and know so much more now than you did when you woke up this morning.'

'I have a question.' Timothy interrupted.

'Go on.'

'How is it I spent the whole day with you and even had a meal with the Elders and when I came back here, it was like time had stood still?'

'Because it did!' Aleobe chuckled. 'When you cross the lines, you cannot exist in two places at once. When you cross to Mielikuvitus, your life here pauses at the exact moment you cross the realm. If you didn't, then your mind would break. The only way that doesn't happen is if something keeps the passageway open.'

The solemn seriousness of Aleobe's answer caught Timothy by surprise and, for a moment, he tried to imagine what that could look like.

'So what can it do, this Nosym?'

'Sky would be the best person to answer that; he's waiting for you if...'

Timothy silenced Aleobe with a suddenly raised hand.

'I'm asking you. Sky, Sucatraps and the Elders they all have an agenda. You, however, you have been my best friend for as long as I can remember. Right now, I'll only listen to you.'

Aleobe remained silent for a moment, and Timothy waited for his friend to answer. Staring through his once again invisible friend, Timothy admired the craftsmanship of the Nosym as he waited for Aleobe to speak.

The little Ecilops' voice was nervous at first, but after clearing his throat with a few coughs, he tried to explain things to Timothy.

'A Partum Spiritus has the power of the mind. All those things you see in your head, all those ideas and random thoughts that burn inside you and feel like train lines running in a million directions. Those things that make you feel so different from everyone else it is your gift.'

'My curse you mean.' Timothy scoffed.

'Yes, mixed within them are visions, but you can see things in your mind in a way other people cannot. When you learn to harness that power, that energy, that insatiable and unstoppable energy, becomes a living thing, it burns.'

'Burns?'

'A Partum Spiritus can create and control the Elemental Flames conjured from their own minds and your Nosym will help focus your mind and allow you to wield and control it.'

'Fire, you expect me to create and control fire?' Timothy's voice was filled with disbelief.

'Sky and Sucatraps can train you to control your mind, tame it and harness it in ways you could never have imagined.'

Timothy felt a sudden blow as he realised how much his imagination had plagued him. Seeing things the way he did, processing things in a way that worked for him had always made him feel the outcast, the unique curiosity on the fringes of "normal" children around him.

Aleobe was there telling him the curse of his isolation was, in fact, a gift and yet Timothy had spent countless nights wishing he could be like all the other children.

'Tell me,' he croaked. 'What is it I see in my dreams?'

'The smoke and eyes?'

'Yes.' Timothy could not hide the fear from his voice. 'What is it and why do I see it?'

'Because you are Partum Spiritus, because you have a connection to Mielikuvitus as only your kind can.'

'But what is it?'

The silence felt awkward as Aleobe fought with himself for how best to answer. He had seen Timothy's reaction when the Elders had told him the nightmares were more than dreams; they were visions. Taking a deep breath, he prepared the best answer he could for Timothy.

'The eyes belong to the reason Sky and the Elders have called on you.' Aleobe began. 'We know it only as the Dark Entity. Who or what it is we aren't sure, but it has re-taken the Shadowlands and is building an army of darkness stronger than we have ever seen.'

'I'm a twelve-year-old boy. What am I supposed to do about it?'

'Age is nothing!' Aleobe snapped. 'You lived in Mielikuvitus for a day and aged less than a minute in your world. You can live and grow a lifetime to prepare. Your age is nothing; your strength of mind means everything.'

Timothy said nothing as he stared at the Nosym. His mind was torn. On one side he wanted to run and on the other he could see sense in what his friend was saying.

'Will you come back?' Aleobe asked, breaking the silence in the room.

'Yes.' Timothy's answer was less than convincing.

But it was an answer, and Aleobe was ready to take him back.

CHAPTER FOURTEEN

DR LIVE'S HOME VISIT

MUCH TO TIMOTHY'S DISMAY, the echo of the door-bell disturbed any further conversation with Aleobe. Hearing the door open, he packed away the box and slid it underneath his bed.

'Can you stay with me or have you got to go back?' He asked as he adjusted the valance sheet to disguise the box.

'I'll stay,' Aleobe answered from the bed. 'I promised Sky I'd either bring you back or come back with an answer. If I tell him you said yes and don't take you back, I think he'll be a little confused.'

The lightness in Aleobe's voice offered Timothy some relief from the fear he had upset his Ecilop friend. He wanted to say a lot more, but as he heard his dad talking to someone at the door, he heard his name mentioned and his ears pricked up.

'Come on, then.' Timothy grinned and sneaked towards his door to open it and earwig on the conversation.

His bedroom was above the front door, on the far side of the landing, allowing him the perfect hideaway to listen to the conversation.

'I'm sorry, were we expecting you?' He heard his dad ask.

'No not at all. I think we discussed a home visit in one of the earlier appointments and I realised I had never followed it through.' Timothy recognised Dr Live's voice and felt a sudden sense of unease. 'I also found a few things I would like to get timothy to try before our next appointment and seeing as your home isn't out of my way, it seemed appropriate. I am sorry if I overstepped.'

'No, not at all.' His mum interrupted, causing Timothy to move back from the edge of the banister to remain unseen. 'Gerard, don't leave the doctor standing on the doorstep.'

'Sorry,' his dad corrected himself. 'Come in. I didn't mean to be rude. Come in.'

'And you, Timothy, you might as well come down instead of listening from the shadows.'

Having been caught out, Timothy's cheeks flushed as he moved rather sheepishly around to the top of the stairs. Still dressed in his school uniform, his unruly red hair looked in need of a trim.

Descending the stairs, he feigned a smile at his mum, who rolled her eyes in response. Feeling uneasy, it relieved him when

95

his mother ruffled his hair as he reached the bottom step and leant in close to whisper to him.

'If you will spy on people, make sure your shadow isn't painted on the wall.'

Casting a quick glance up the stairs, Timothy once again blushed as he realised how obvious he had been by leaving his bedroom door open when he had snuck out to listen. To his relief, his mum saw the funny side and wrapped her arm across his shoulder.

'Good evening Timothy,' the pointy-faced doctor grinned. 'Sorry to catch you off-guard like this. I just wanted to give you some things that might help before I see you next.'

Removing himself from his mother's hug, he stepped off the bottom step and past the mirror. Not chancing a glance toward the glass, he focussed on Dr Live and reached out to take the curious bundle she held in her hand. She handed him what felt like a book wrapped in brown paper and secured with twine.

'This is a journal. I want you to use it to write your thoughts, feelings, worries, dreams and keep a record of the things that cause you concern during the day.' Her warm smile filled him with encouragement as he turned over the wrapped book and peeled away the paper. 'There's nothing you can't put in there and it will be between just the two of us.'

'What if Aiden finds it?' Timothy asked as he pulled the book free of the wrapping.

'Then you'd better hide it in a very good place, so he doesn't.' Dr Live answered with a coy smile and a sly wink. 'All those things you see in your imagination, the places, the dreams and everything else I want you to write in there.'

'Like homework?'

'Like fun homework, so make it interesting.' She smiled again and as he was about to answer, the doctor's attention was drawn to the mirror mounted on the wall.

For a moment, the doctor seemed entranced by the ornate mirror. Stepping past Timothy, she moved to stand in front of the glass and peered at the three broken segments in the corners.

'Amazing.' She gasped as she removed a set of spectacles from her pocket and perched them on her nose. 'Such beautiful craftsmanship, look at the work on the crest.'

Standing on her tiptoes, she peered at the open-winged bird that sat atop a faded shield, holding it in its claws as if in mid-flight. The bird had always unnerved Timothy, but the doctor seemed almost drawn to the intricate wooden carving.

'I'm sorry!' Dr Live announced, snatching her attention from the mirror and back to her hosts. 'I'm a collector of antiques, and I have seen nothing so exquisite as this.'

'It's just a mirror.' Timothy remarked and felt a sharp jab in his shoulder from his father, who was now standing next to him.

'Oh, it is much more than that, isn't that right, Mr Scott?' The doctor's words seemed a little off to Timothy, but he could not place why.

'It's been in our family for generations. The kids think it's ugly, but I remember my grandparents having it hanging in their hallway when I was Cathy's age.'

'I see that it has seen better days.' The doctor leaned in closer to inspect the cracked glass in the bottom-left corner panel. 'How did this happen?'

There was a definite pause before his dad answered. Timothy felt uncomfortable with the unexpected change in the air as the doctor continued to inspect the mirror with renewed interest.

'These things happen over the years, adds to the character.' His dad explained, his voice somehow hoarse.

'How much?'

'I beg your pardon?'

'To buy it, I'd love to fix it up and display it in all its glory.' Dr Live ran her thin fingers along the frame of the mirror.

'I'm sorry,' his dad began. 'Like I said, it's been in my family for generations and I'd never think of parting with it, sorry.'

For a split second, the doctor's face contorted with irritation, but she replaced her mask with haste. Giving the mirror one last look, she removed the glasses and turned to face the family.

'I didn't mean to be rude,' she corrected and removed a business card from her jacket pocket. 'You find treasures such as these so rarely, it's hard not to let the collector in me get carried away.'

Every inch the warm and caring doctor, once again she held out the small card for his mother to take.

'That's my personal contact details. Should you change your mind now or any time? I would hate to miss the opportunity to have something so rare and so beautiful.'

'Rare?' Timothy's mum asked as she looked at the business card.

'Oh yes, I have only ever seen one such mirror like this in all my years. It was in a Stately Home in Finland. It caught my imagination even as a child. It could be worth a lot of money.'

Dr Live allowed her words to linger for a moment, as if testing how far she could push towards a sale. The lack of response told her everything, and she cast aside her genuine interest as a collector of antiquities and returned to her proper role as Timothy's doctor.

'I fear I really have overstepped now. I shall take my leave and allow you to enjoy the evening in peace.'

Moving to the front door, she cast Timothy one last look and nodded her head to the journal he now held in his hands.

'Don't forget, fill the pages with your imagination and realise how powerful it is.' She offered him a warm smile as she opened the door.

'Thank you,' Timothy smiled. 'I promise I will.'

Seeing herself out of the front door, the hallway was eerie and quiet as Timothy stood with his parents, a little taken aback by what had just happened.

'Well, that was different,' his dad chuckled as he took the business card from Susan. 'I don't think we'll need this.'

'She's an odd one. I'll give her that.' His mum smiled and turned to go back into the living room, leaving Timothy alone.

Making sure he was alone, Timothy moved to stand in front of the mirror and felt his heart skip a beat as he saw Aleobe perched once again on his shoulder. Knowing he could not see the Ecilop if he took his eyes away from the reflection, he waited for his friend to speak.

'I agree with your mum. She is an odd one.' Aleobe laughed. 'Seemed interested in the mirror, though.'

'Do you think she knows what it can do?' Timothy asked, his voice filled with concern.

'Not a chance. She just wants it because it's worth money. That's always been the problem with your world. People bother with cost, value and money.'

'I suppose.' Timothy agreed. 'So, when can I come back?'

Timothy watched as Aleobe cast his gaze around the hallway, as if making sure they were alone. That brought a smile to Timothy's face as he realised, regardless of anything, Aleobe was invisible to everyone.

'When everyone is asleep, I will take you back,' Aleobe smiled. 'That is if you're still willing to come back?'

'Yes, I am.'

Unlike before, when they had been disturbed by the doorbell, Timothy's answer was now resolute and filled with determination.

CHAPTER FIFTEEN

GOING BACK

I T TOOK FOREVER TO pass through the evening, or at least it felt that way to Timothy. After eating, they all worked on their homework and settled down for a few matches of Mario Kart on the TV downstairs before bed. Mum settled Cathy in bed earlier than the boys and the usual rivalry had ensued.

After a handful of lost games, Aiden was showing his frustration and soon dropped the controller onto the sofa as yet another race ended with him in last position.

'I hate this guy,' he had sulked much to the amusement of his dad, who mocked him with a stuck out bottom lip.

'Come on then guys, it's that time again. Go get yourselves ready for bed.'

Aiden had been about to protest, but Timothy was glad to have been dismissed for the evening. With no ritual repeat from his dad followed by veiled threats of "no games tomorrow" or "if you don't get a move on we won't be going out at the weekend" Timothy bolted up the stairs.

In fact, before Aiden had even entered the bathroom to wash and brush his teeth, Timothy was halfway across the landing towards his own room.

'What's gotten into you?' Aiden scoffed as he turned on the bathroom light.

'I'm just tired is all, night.'

Without waiting for a reply, Timothy shot into his room and jumped into his bed. He had just finished adjusting his alarm clock, setting it for the middle of the night, when his parents came in. Sharing their usual pre-bed routines, Timothy was plunged into darkness and for the first time was eager to fall asleep. It was lost on him. He had not even considered the foreboding shadow and eyes as he normally would. Instead, he welcomed dreams and sleep with eagerness.

It took a few moments to register the muted vibrations underneath his pillow. At last, when his tired brain understood what it was, Timothy's eyes opened, and he reached into the pillowcase to mute the alarm.

'Glad you're awake.' Aleobe's voice hushed from his bedside table. 'I was tempted to wake you but thought it best not to.'

'Have my parents gone to bed?' Timothy asked as he sat up in bed and looked around the dark bedroom.

The light from outside poured in through a strategic crack in the curtains. It gave him enough light to make out the main hazards in the room and the pile of clothes he had put aside for when he awoke.

Moving with great care so as not to rouse anyone else in the house, Timothy dressed in warmer bedclothes and moved to his bedroom door.

Opening it with caution, he peeked into the landing. He was pleased to see the nightlight was switched off and his parent's bedroom door was closed. They were the two telltale signs he was alone and everyone else was asleep.

Pulling on a pair of slippers, he moved out into the hallway.

'To the mirror, I guess?' He asked Aleobe as he walked around to the top of the staircase.

'Yes,' Timothy was about to take the first step when Aleobe stopped him. 'Wait!'

'What is it?' Timothy snapped as he looked around, afraid he would see his sister staring at them.

'The box and your Nosym. Have you got it?'

Rolling his eyes, Timothy turned around and tiptoed back to his bedroom door. Drawing the curtains open an inch further, he turned around and moved to reach under the bed. In no time at all, he had the box secure under his arm and once again moved to the door.

'Anything else before we get going this time?'

'Nope, think we've got it all *this time*!'

Timothy smiled at Aleobe's obvious glee that Timothy had agreed to return to Mielikuvitus. Moving in silence, the pair descended the stairs and moved to stand in front of the mirror.

'So,' Timothy started as he adjusted the box underneath his arm. 'How does this all work, then? Magic words or what?'

'Nothing like that Timothy,' Aleobe grinned as he looked at Timothy from his reflection in the mirror. 'You just have to want to cross. That's why I asked you in the first place if you wanted to see me.'

'I want to go b...'

A shuffling noise caught both their attention, and they turned to look for the source of the sudden noise. It had sounded like someone dragging their feet across the wooden floor of the kitchen, but Timothy couldn't be sure.

Stepping away from the mirror, Timothy placed the Nosym box on the bottom step and crept towards the kitchen door. Inching the door open, Timothy could hear his heart pounding in his ears as he peeked into the empty room.

Nothing moved or seemed out of place. Everything in the kitchen was still except for a curtain that wafted in a gentle breeze. Feeling the relief, Timothy pushed the door and wedged it with the rubber doorstop they used.

Crossing the kitchen, he reached over the worktop and pulled the window behind the curtain closed. Lowering the handle, he secured it and turned around to look back into the hallway.

'Not like mum and dad to leave the windows open, they must have been tired.'

Although it seemed odd that his father, a security-conscious man who checked, re-checked and triple-checked the doors before bed, Timothy had grander things on his mind. Leaving the kitchen door wedged open, Timothy walked back into the hallway and retrieved the Nosym box.

As he busied himself around the mirror, he had failed to see the shrouded figure hidden behind the kitchen door.

Dressed all in black, the slender figure had been the one responsible for leaving the window open, as it had been their means of entering the sleeping house.

Dressed all in black, the figure had no distinguishing features. Like a prowling cat, they chanced their own look around the door to see what Timothy was up to. Seeing the young boy standing in front of the mirror, they watched for a moment before stepping out from behind the door and skulk across to the shadow beneath the stairs.

Timothy saw nothing of the intruder's movements. Something fixed his attention on the mirror and the reflection staring back at him. At first, as before, nothing was different about the representation of himself looking back through the glass. The reflection was just that. A mirror copy of him holding the box stood in the cold hallway.

'Are you ready?' Aleobe asked as Timothy felt the excitement grow inside him.

'Yes.'

As if to answer, the reflection twitched and then turned its head from side-to-side as if stretching from a long slumber. After a few rotations of its shoulders, the reflection offered Timothy a welcoming nod. After a second, he returned the gesture.

Unlike before, the reflection of Timothy seemed curious about something beyond Timothy and turned its attention to the staircase beside the mirror. Following the reflection's gaze, Timothy looked to the dark shadows beneath the staircase but saw nothing in the dark hallway.

'Probably nothing,' he said aloud, more to comfort himself than anything else.

Timothy returned his attention to the mirror, and his reflection turned to face him.

No sooner had the reflection returned its attention to Timothy than did it once again look away towards the staircase. Raising its hand, the reflection tapped its finger against the inside of the mirror as if pointing towards the stairs.

Taking that as the sign to move, Timothy raised his hand and touched his own finger to the glass, where his reflection was doing the same. As soon as he felt the cold glass against his skin, the reflection snatched its head around to look at him, a look of terror clear on its face.

'NO!' His own voice hissed as the reflection slapped its free hand against the inside of the mirror.

Fear enveloped Timothy as he turned his head to see the slender figure emerge from the shadows, dressed all in black. It was too late to do anything, as his reflection was powerless to resist, and reached through the glass to take hold of his wrist.

As the burglar lunged forward to take hold of Timothy, he was ripped from where he stood and dragged once again into the mirror and across the divide into Mielikuvitus. Still holding the box, he waited for when he arrived and felt the soft earth beneath his feet.

Feeling himself land he opened his eyes and ignored the wave of nausea that washed over him.

'Who was that?' He gasped, looking around for Aleobe.

'I don't know,' the Ecilop replied as he flexed his purple wings and launched into the air. 'But we need to work out how we will get you back if they're waiting for you when you return.'

Any feeling of excitement that Timothy had felt about returning was now overshadowed by the fear of who, or what, had lunged for him from the shadows in the hallway.

Chapter Sixteen

Walking A New Path

Timothy was more than happy to see Sucatraps and Sky waiting for him. He had arrived at the same place as before, in the open glade on the banks of the Rainbow River. The sound of cascading water filled the air, and he felt the peacefulness of his surroundings.

Taking in a deep breath, he could almost taste the sweetness in the air and he closed his eyes for a moment. The worry of the intruder seemed far less important as he allowed himself to absorb the majesty of Mielikuvitus.

Aside from the tumbling water over the rocks, he could hear the wind rustling through the pastel-coloured leaves of the forest on the far side of the river. The song of birds carried in the wind, but he could not pinpoint where they were. After another deep breath, he opened his eyes.

'It has that effect, even for those of us who live here.' Sky beamed as he turned from the river to face Timothy. 'Especially here. There's something peaceful about the Mystic Forest.'

'I am glad you have decided to come back?' Sucatraps interrupted, throwing him a wry, knowing smile as she turned to look at him.

Once again, she was dressed in yet another garment. This was a mauve dress that dragged on the grass behind her as she walked. Once again, Sucatraps was aided by the crooked cane and Timothy chuckled as he saw the oversized magnifying glass tucked into a hessian belt that wrapped around her waist.

'Were my clothes not good enough for you?' Sucatraps scoffed as she pointed to the clothes from home Timothy was wearing.

It was the first time he realised that the fine garments and side-slung cloak had disappeared when he had returned from the Table Of Haras.

'I didn't take them home with me.' He stammered, his brow furrowed with slight confusion. 'In fact, I don't know where they are.'

'Unless you take something with you purposefully, the journey will always return you as you were when you left.' Sky explained as he pointed to the box still wedged beneath Timothy's arm. 'You intended to bring your Nosym with you!'

Timothy was about to speak when Sucatraps silenced him with her wrinkled hand.

'Not so fast,' she interrupted. 'You're here now, by choice, and you *will* dress in the proper manner.'

Sucatraps stepped forward and tapped the tip of her cane into Timothy's waist. In response, he felt the clothes he was wearing change. Somehow, the light nightclothes were replaced with the lighter fabric of the black and silver-stitched trousers. Still in awe of the magic of Mielikuvitus, he waited for the feeling to pass before admiring the finely crafted clothes he was once again wearing.

'Better!' Sucatraps laughed and offered Sky the podium to once again speak.

'You understand what it means, having agreed to come back?' Sky asked as Timothy toyed with the cape hanging over his right arm.

'I think so.'

'Thinking so is not the right answer.' Sky corrected. 'You are here to learn the ways of your ancestors, to accept your place as a Partum Spiritus and face the darkness.'

'Aleobe explained some bits to me,' Timothy answered in a quiet voice. 'I have some questions, though.'

'It would be a concern if you didn't have questions.' Sky smirked, his canine eyes scanning the landscape around them for a moment. 'Blindly accepting a quest and fate such as this is nothing short of stupidity.'

'I have things to do,' Sucatraps interjected, as she unfurled a small scroll from her pocket and read the writing on the sheet. 'If I may be excused, I have a wedding to prepare for?'

'Timothy?' Sky looked at him for an answer.

'I'm the guest here,' Timothy stammered. 'Do what you need to do. Sorry for keeping you waiting.'

For a moment, Timothy wasn't sure how the old woman would respond. Her face changed from its playful look to one more serious. After a few unsure moments, she offered him her answer.

'Timothy, forget who and what you are in your world. We have seen your people, their cruelty and scorn, when someone sits apart from their normality. In Mielikuvitus you are not a twelve-year-old boy, you are not a stranger or curiosity. You are a Partum Spiritus, you are here to protect our way of life, so please, please forget what insecurities you have in your world and realise how important you are to us here.'

The old woman took his hand in hers and Timothy felt a lump in his throat. Sucatraps spoke with kindness and pride as she stared into his eyes.

'My boy, you are stronger than you allow yourself to believe.'

Releasing his hand, he watched as the old woman offered Sky a nod and disappeared before his eyes. There was a lot Timothy needed to get used to, least of all the curious nature of Mieliku-vitus and the ability of some to evaporate before his eyes.

'What say we take a walk and I will try to answer some of your questions?' Sky interrupted his thoughts. 'Your friend is also welcome to come.'

Aleobe had been perched on a damp rock watching a variety of fish swim beneath the glassy surface of Rainbow River.

Hearing himself being mentioned, he snatched his head around and accepted Timothy's signal to join the pair as they walked. Without hesitation the Ecilop launched himself backwards off the damp rock and flew to hover by his friend's side.

As a trio, Timothy followed Sky's lead as they walked along the banks of the Rainbow River, keeping the Mystic Forest to their right and Partum City, off in the distance, behind them.

'So, Timothy, what do you want to know?'

They walked and talked for a long time. Timothy had pressed Sky about the Dark Entity that Aleobe had mentioned when trying to explain the smoky-red-eyed creature of his nightmares. It had taken some time for Timothy to understand what Sky was saying to him, but as they reached a slow bend in the meandering river; he thought he understood what Sky had explained to him.

'What you're saying,' Timothy began as he tried to summarise what he had been told. 'Is that since the last time the darkness was fought by my ancestors, there has been peace. That is until recently, when something has awoken the darkness and taken the form I see in my dreams?'

'Visions, they are not dreams.' Sky corrected him. 'That is the Dark Entity's attempt to communicate with you. To fill you with fears and nightmares and keep you from facing him.'

'He's doing a good job.' Timothy confessed.

'It is in its nature to feed on fear and where fear cannot be found, it plants it and nurtures its growth in whatever mind it touches. You are a threat to its existence, to its growth, and it knows that.'

'Why do you say it and not he or she?'

'When the Dark Entity came into being, it gave up the life it had before. Being so consumed by the lingering malcontent, anger and darkness in the Shadowlands, it became a thing of the dark. It has no presence other than evil.'

Sky's words were laced with frustration and Timothy sensed how uncomfortable his questioning was making his guide. That said, however, these were things he believed he needed to know. Oddly, he trusted that Sky would answer his questions as long as he needed him to.

'Where is it now?'

'The Dark Entity?'

'Yes, I'm guessing the Shadowlands are a big place and you can't expect me to learn whatever it is you're planning on teaching me and hunt for this thing at the same time?'

'Not at all!' Sky stopped and turned to look out across the landscape.

Timothy had not realised they had walked away from the banks of the river. For some time, they had been following a small stream that had etched a path through the land at the side of an immense hill. Having ascended what appeared to be a steep hill via a winding path, he could now see Mielikuvitus from an elevated perspective.

Looking behind them, Timothy could see the path they had taken along the zigzagging path of the tumbling stream. Looking at it, he realised why he had not felt the steepness of the climb as it meandered along the contours of the hill.

Further than he had expected, he could make out the Rainbow River below them and for the first time saw the shimmering colours beneath the surface of the water as they caught the sunlight.

Turning, Timothy looked around and settled his attention on an impressive range of jagged mountains. As he climbed the rest of the hill in silence, the view opened up before him until he could see the curious beauty of the Torn Mountains.

Two ranges of mountains were split either side of a wide valley. The hill he was on stood aligned to the valley and allowed Timothy to see beyond the Torn Mountains, and what Sky explained were the Shadowlands.

'The Torn Mountains you see in front of you stretch almost from shore to shore across the width of the land.' Sky explained as he moved to sit on a rock at the top of the hill. Waiting for Timothy to join him, he continued his explanation of the view. 'Those on the left give passage to the Narrows and Forgottenlands, a place we do not venture to.'

'And that, the dark place in the distance?' Timothy suspected he knew the answer.

The area he was talking of was a place beyond the valley, shrouded in heavy clouds. Even from their distance on the far side of the mountain range, Timothy could see the brewing storm and the occasional flicker of lightning crackling between the black clouds.

'That is why you won't need to search for the Dark Entity.' Sky answered after a few moment's silence. 'If you look, you will see water beneath the clouds.'

Squinting, as if that would help, Timothy tried to make out what Sky was talking about. Between a flash of lightning, he could see the reflection of water far off in the distance.

'That is Shadow Island, an old fortified island in the middle of the Black Lake.' Sky explained. 'That is where the Dark Entity is. It is where you will face it and stop it from corrupting Mielikuvitus and spreading darkness to the worlds beyond this one.'

Suddenly, the weight of what they expected of him troubled Timothy.

Sky allowed Timothy the time to watch the rumbling storm clouds far off in the distance. It was impossible to judge distance and yet Timothy felt the storm was closer than he would like it to have been. Framed between the jagged valley in the Torn Mountains, Timothy felt very much unprepared for what lay ahead.

CHAPTER SEVENTEEN

PLAYING WITH FIRE

T HE JOURNEY BACK FROM the hilltop to the Rainbow River was quiet and uneventful. Timothy was haunted by his first view of the Shadowlands and Sky left him alone to ponder his thoughts.

Upon reaching the bottom of the hill Timothy was glad to see the mound in the earth obscured his view of the valley and storm clouds. He could see nothing beyond the peaks of the Torn Mountains. Although he could no longer see them, the icy cold feeling that the Shadowlands had caused still felt fresh on his skin.

'We need to discuss some things Timothy, if you will?'

Sky's voice dragged him back in an instant and Timothy re-alised he had reached the banks of the river. Lost in thought he had been staring into the turbulent water. Turning around, he found Aleobe and Sky sat at a wooden table outside a grand tent that looked to be made of stitched leaves.

'Sorry,' Timothy apologised as he tried to recall if he had noticed the tent as he had walked back. 'What did you say?'

The foreboding views haunted him like a bad dream, a feeling he was all too familiar with. Doing his best to cast it aside he moved to the table and took a seat on a stool that appeared to have grown from the ground.

'We need to discuss how you will move on from this moment.' Sky began. 'The task ahead of you is no easy feat; we will test you beyond anything you could imagine preparing you.'

Timothy noted the serious tone to Sky's words and paid absolute attention to what he was saying.

'For the moment, I have suggested to Aleobe and Sucatraps that we begin the training here by the river. It is, after all, the place you seem most drawn to.'

'How is that?'

'When I offered you passage to Mielikuvitus, it is you who decides where you arrive, not me.' Aleobe explained. 'Both times, your soul seemed drawn to the river's banks. Because of that, Sky thinks it would be best if we started your training here. In a place you seem to have a connection with.'

'You're the ones in charge,' Timothy shrugged. 'I'll do as I am told.'

'It will take more than obedience.' Sky boomed and moved with frightening speed.

Leaping over the table, Sky somersaulted over Timothy's head and landed on the grass behind him. The sudden gymnastic agility and prowess of Sky's acrobatics stunned Timothy. Trying to understand what had just happened, he caught Sky's now serious gaze.

Mouth agape, Timothy turned in his seat struggling to form a sentence in response to what had just happened. As Sky's cape settled back into position, draped over both shoulders, he pointed to the Nosym box that sat on the grass beside Timothy's stool.

'Open it and take the Nosym.'

Sky waited as Timothy opened the box with great care and scooped up the bound wood and crystal Nosym. It surprised Timothy how warm the Nosym felt in his hand. Admiring the craftsmanship, his fingers wrapped around the shaft and fit perfect into the grooves created from the binding.

'What you wield in your hand goes by many names. Each one is crafted by the generation before its owner. This was made for you when you were born and has waited with the Elders for the day you needed it.' Sky explained as Timothy admired the curiosity in his hand.

'What does it do?'

'May I?' Sky walked up to him and held out his hands.

Timothy handed his guide the Nosym and waited as Sky weighed the item in his hand. Wrapping both hands around the bound grip, it looked thin in his hands. As if testing the weight, Sky twisted the Nosym this way, and that. After testing the Nosym he closed his eyes and took a long, deep breath in.

'Partum Spiritus are the only true people who can wield these weapons.'

Sky explained everything to Timothy as he took a handful of deep breaths to focus his concentration.

'There are but a few of us, myself and Sucatraps being two, that were taught the basics of how to wield it. Just enough to help teach new generations of Partum Spiritus.'

Timothy watched entranced as Sky opened his eyes and stared off into the distance. Grasping the Nosym in both hands, Sky's concentration was intense as he fought to take control of the curious item in his hands.

'Your Nosym allows you to focus your power, concentrate your energy on a single point. When you have that, you can then manipulate and control it, shape and contain it.' Sky took one last deep breath. 'Like this!'

Timothy's mouth went wider as a line of flames emerged from both crystal ends of the Nosym. Contained within some invisible force field, the flames burned bright until they stretched out as far as necessary before they curved inwards and a thin, almost invisible string of fire connected the tips of the two bow limbs of flame.

Timothy admired the flaming bow that Sky now wielded in his right hand.

'The Partum Spiritus can control the eternal flame that burns within them and use it to create anything they desire.'

Sky scooped the bowstring of fire in the crooks of his three fingers and pulled it back. As the string pulled taught, an arrow of fire appeared. The burning arrow was latched onto the string and rested against the grip of the Nosym.

'Weapons and ammunition, all at the beck and call of the tamed mind.' Sky continued and loosed the arrow out towards the Rainbow River.

The burning arrow left a thin trail of smoke behind it as it flew. The arrow took Timothy's attention, and he watched its flight until it splashed into the turbulent surface of the river. The roar of the water drowned out the *hiss* as fire met water, but that was forgotten as Sky's demonstration was far from over.

'From bows to swords.' Sky announced as Timothy returned his attention to his host.

Changing his grip, now wielding the Nosym in both hands, Sky drew it up through the air. The bowstring disappeared, and the lower limb did the same. The upper limb took on a new appearance as the shaft of fire grew thicker and a prominent point formed at the tip of what was now a broadsword blade.

Sky wielded the cumbersome weapon with ease, dragging the burning blade this way and that through the air, leaving a trail of black smoke in its wake.

'If not for swords, perhaps an axe.'

The fire changed again. The pointed tip of the sword materialising into the wide shaft of an axe-face as Sky drew it through the air and sliced the seat where Timothy had been sitting. Stepping back, Timothy stared at the two smouldering halves.

'What else?' Timothy panted like an excited dog.

'A club?' Sky offered and the axe-head changed. 'A double-edged sword, perhaps?'

Once again, the weapon changed and two wide blades formed, one from either end of the Nosym. Sky rotated and balanced the blades in both hands until he had gained enough momentum to rotate the spinning blades high above his head.

'Or it can be a tool of construction,' the fire-blades evaporated, and the Nosym took on the appearance of a sledgehammer.

'How are you doing that?' Timothy asked, in awe of what Sky was doing.

'I learned long ago under the tutelage of your ancestors how to manipulate the Eternal Flame.' Sky explained as he drew the flame back into the gaping maw of the snake and lion. 'I cannot control it as the Partum Spiritus can, but I know enough. Enough to show you what you are capable of and the power you have.'

Sky looked drained, his skin looked pallid and pale as he handed Timothy back the Nosym. Relieving himself of the burden, Sky staggered back to the table and leant himself against it to catch his breath.

'Give him a minute.' Aleobe declared as Timothy moved to speak to Sky. 'None of that comes natural to him. It takes a lot of effort to do what he has just done. Let him recover a moment.'

Timothy watched as Sky fought to catch his breath and wiped the beads of sweat from his forehead. Looking beyond exhausted, Sky moved around the table and staggered his way across to the flapping doors of the pastel-coloured tent. Pulling aside the opening, he staggered inside without a word.

Timothy remained on the banks of the river with Aleobe, a look of concern painted on his face.

'Will he be OK?' Timothy asked as he returned the Nosym into the box and lifted it onto the table.

'He just needs a little time.' Aleobe comforted, but as Timothy secured the lid of the box, the Ecilop cast a concerned glance back at the tent. 'What do you say we watch the sunset and enjoy the beauty of Mielikuvitus?'

Timothy wasn't sure. The hypnotic feat of magic and fire he had just witnessed had sparked a thousand questions in his head. He wanted to learn more, to learn to do what Sky had done, but he had seen the effect it had had on him.

With the smell of burnt wood thick in the air as he stood next to the smouldering seat, Timothy accepted his friend's offer. As the sun descended towards the distant horizon, the friends stood by the banks of the river. Together, they watched as the golden rays of the dying sun painted the hues of blues, greens and purples of the trees in a brilliant new light.

'I'd never thought something like this was possible.' Timothy gasped as the leaves changed from light to dark as if preparing for the night.

'You have seen nothing yet,' Aleobe said as he sat perched on his friend's shoulder. 'You are part of this world now. There is much for you to see.'

CHAPTER EIGHTEEN

FROM THE LION

IMOTHY SAW NO SIGN of Sky after his demonstration. After a long walk with Aleobe, as the magnificent sunset bathed the open grassland on the banks of the Rainbow River, they returned to the camp to find a fire burning and the tent was silent. They had sat around the fire until the blanket of stars flickered to life. Soon tiredness washed over them and they thought it best to retire.

Entering the tent, it surprised Timothy to find a set of steps leading down under the ground. Having expected to find a normal tent interior, the fact the tent covered a passage underground was somewhat of a surprise. Following the steps down, a series of rooms had been burrowed into the ground much like a rabbit's warren.

Aleobe had shown him the room that had been saved for him. Timothy was glad to find a bed on the mossy floor waiting for him. Lying on top of the soft sheets, sleep came and, for the first time in a long time, he was swallowed by a dreamless sleep.

The sense of someone watching woke Timothy the following morning. Having fallen asleep fully dressed, he opened his eyes to find Sky stood looking down at him.

'Quiet.' Sky hissed in the dim room, illuminated only by a dying candle on the bedside table. 'Follow me and bring the Nosym.'

Leaving before Timothy could answer, he wiped the sleep from his eyes and swung his legs over the edge of the bed. Looking around the room, it relieved him to find the boxed Nosym sat next to the dying candle. He lifted the lid and retrieved the wood and crystal weapon before leaving the small burrow-room.

Emerging from the bedroom, Timothy caught sight of Sky as he ascended the stairs and hurried across the open space to catch him.

'Where are we going?' He asked as he reached Sky's side, but his guide remained silent.

Stepping through the doors of the tent, Timothy was surprised to find the world still swallowed in darkness. The horizon was showing signs of first light, but the blanket of stars still twinkled high above. Stepping into the early morning air, Timothy felt the chill against his skin and shivered.

'What time is it?' Timothy asked as he followed Sky towards the rumbling river.

'Early' was his short answer. 'This is how it will be for some time.'

Reaching the river's edge, Sky scooped his hands into the flowing water and washed with the colourful liquid. Cupping his hands, he sipped a mouthful of water before wiping his lips with the back of his hand.

'Are you ready to train?' Sky asked as he stood and turned to face him.

'Yes.'

'It is my intention to show you what you are capable of,' Sky explained. 'You will face trials both physical and mental. Your body will fight you, but you must push through this and accept who and what you are.'

'I'm ready.'

A sly smile appeared on Sky's face as he nodded at what Timothy had said.

'You're ready, are you?' Sky chuckled. 'I'll be the judge of that.'

They centred the whole of the morning on Timothy, calming his mind and focus his concentration. Although he longed to discover how to make the flames erupt from the gaping mouths of the crystal figures on the Nosym, Sky had no intention of focussing on this.

Having sensed Timothy's eagerness, and associated frustration, the whole day was spent testing Timothy with daunting exercises and then forcing him to calm his racing heart.

Although Sky explained that he needed to first control his own body and mind before he could dream of controlling the eternal flame, Timothy was still a twelve-year-old boy. Filled with an insatiable curiosity and yearning to run before he could walk, he pressed to be allowed to try to conjure the flames from the ends of the Nosym.

'Please, at least tell me how.' Timothy begged as he swallowed the last mouthful of his lunch. 'Then I can practise.'

Sky sighed as he took a long drink, but knew the young boy would not relent on his requests until he had shown him his limitations.

'Fine.' Sky sighed. 'Come with me.'

'Can I finish this first?' Timothy asked as he pointed to the food left on the plate.

'Now or never.' Sky snapped as he rose and stalked across the wide open plain of grass behind the tent.

Sky beckoned for Timothy to join him in the centre of a circle of stones in the grass. Stuffing the last mouthful of food into his mouth, he chewed as he stepped into the circle to join Sky.

'These stones will contain the flame, should you even manage to call it? No matter what happens, the fire will not breach the circle and everything around us will be safe.'

'Is it that dangerous?' Timothy asked, aware of how nervous he was.

'Yes, but you wanted to experience it and I think you need to see what can happen if you do not tame your mind.'

Sky positioned Timothy in the centre of the stone ring and moved to a safer position on the other side of the stones. Checking their surroundings, Sky gave him instructions and waited for Timothy to do as he was told.

'Take the Nosym in your strong hand and close your eyes.' Sky waited as Timothy followed his instructions. 'Make sure the lion points to the sky and the snake to the ground.'

Opening his eyes, Timothy flipped over the Nosym and ensured he could see the snarling mouth of the lion pointing up towards the cloudy sky. Happy that it was now in the correct position, he once again closed his eyes.

'Quiet your mind and listen to my words.'

Sky's calm voice talked him through a mantra of relaxation. At first, stood in the middle of an open field, Timothy felt ridiculous and self-conscious. Being told to calm his breathing and feel the flow of air around him sounded like something his mum had tried when he had first started having the nightmares.

'Concentrate on what I am saying.' Sky barked as Timothy's mind had wandered to his home and family. 'If you can't quieten your mind, you will never find what we are looking for.'

'What are we looking for?' Timothy snapped and opened his eyes to glare at Sky in frustration. 'You're telling me to relax and calm myself and I don't even know what you're expecting me to feel or find?'

'Anger will not get you control, Timothy.' Sky soothed. 'Your mind and body need to be calm. You need to be in control.'

'Right.' Timothy huffed and closed his eyes again.

Sky repeated the mantra as he had before, guiding Timothy into a state of relaxation by feeding off the sounds and smells of the world around him. Although his mind tried to fight his attempts to relax, Timothy soon started to shut out the niggling voice in the back of his mind. Slowly, all he could feel and hear was the gentle breeze and the distant sound of running water.

Sky's voice sounded distant now. His words were nothing more than a whispered guide, almost drowned out by the sounds of nature around him. As the deep sense of relaxation settled inside him, Timothy felt something different.

It was hard to explain and had he been asked to, he doubted he could have found the words for what he felt. In the deepest pit of his stomach, he felt a sensation of warmth that grew into a physical heat. As that feeling grew, it was as if the heat was pulsing, sending waves of warmth flowing through his body.

As his awareness of it grew, he heard Sky's voice, distant and mellow, telling him to channel the heat into his strong hand.

'Think of it as a flowing stream. While there may be many branches and paths it may take, it is for you to direct it where you want it to go.'

In his mind's eye, Timothy siphoned the heat, blocking off avenues where it could escape. Forcing it to flow towards his outstretched hand and the Nosym held in it. After what felt like an age, his body grew tired, but he was determined to succeed.

After a time, the pulsing heat seemed to only be focussed in three distinct places. Whereas it had consumed his entire body, it was now only in the pit of his stomach, in his slow-beating heart, and along the length of his right arm.

'When you are ready, when you know the strength flows only where you want, you can open your eyes.'

Uncertain of how much control he had, Timothy opened his eyes and felt relief as the heat remained present in the same places.

'Focus on the Nosym, look at the lion. Examine the detail of the craftsmanship, the teeth, the eyes, the fur and see it not only physically but also in the depths of your imagination.'

'I see it.'

'Now picture the heat flowing from you to the Nosym. Control it though, as you did when you channelled it,' Sky was nervous as he watched from outside the ring of stones. 'Remember, you are in control.'

Sky watched as Timothy's brow furrowed with concentration as he fought to siphon the primal power building inside him. Sky knew what would happen, for all his eagerness he knew that Timothy was not ready. That being said, however, he knew the only way for Timothy to learn was to experience it for himself.

As he stood in the centre of the ring, Timothy focussed everything on the jagged teeth in the giant maw of the crystal lion. He pictured the heat pouring through him and into the shaft of the Nosym. His fingers grew warmer, or perhaps it was the wood absorbing the heat from within him, until he could see a flicker of light in the depths of the lion's mouth.

His excitement grew as the light grew brighter until, without warning, a beam of fire exploded from the lion's mouth. At first, the fire spat out in a burst, spraying globules of molten flame on the surrounding ground. Forcing himself to concentrate more, Timothy fought to take control of the flame but as the spitting flames intensified, so did the heat coursing through him.

What was once warmth had become a searing heat that continued to rise. Timothy's furrowed brow gave way to a look of concern and then fear.

'What's happening?' He yelled as his arm and the Nosym became enveloped in unbearable heat. 'Help me.'

Sky watched. He knew no harm would come to Timothy and that the boy needed to experience what was about to happen.

As the heat intensified, the spraying flames became a fountain of fire. The end of the Nosym sparked like an out-of-control firework and, try as he might, Timothy could not release the wooden handle from his hand. As the fountain intensified, the flame reached the edge of the stone ring but passed no further than its boundary.

The flames exploded into the air until, without warning, the flames took on a physical form. The roaring fire had a mind of its own now and took on the appearance of a lion that towered over Timothy. At least thirty-feet tall, the lion's face looked around until its focus turned on Timothy.

'You are not one to hold the power.'

The voice it was familiar. He knew it all too well from his dreams.

'Please.' Timothy begged.

As the plea left his lips, the flames extinguished, and all that was left was a cloud of black smoke where the fire had burned. Timothy stared at the mass of black smoke until a pair of burning red reptilian eyes opened in the cloud.

'No!' Timothy shrieked as the eyes bore down on him.

The eyes of his nightmare glared down at him and his body went cold with fear.

As the terror took over him, the world closed in around him. Timothy lost all control of his senses. The last thing he remembered as he slumped to the floor was Sky's voice booming out and the black cloud evaporating into the air.

Unconsciousness swallowed Timothy as the world faded and he lost all awareness of anything around him.

CHAPTER NINETEEN

THE LIVING MAP

I NSIDE THE CONFINES OF the underground room, Timothy opened his eyes and gasped for air. Someone had changed him into more comfortable clothes, but they were now drenched in sweat. The nightmare had come again. The image of the towering cloud of black smoke where the burning lion had been haunted him.

The vision, the Dark Entity, as Aleobe had named it, had spoken again. Its words remained the same, yet now they echoed with a sinister air. It was as if it somehow knew he had defied its warning and now roamed the lands of Mielikuvitus.

'You've been asleep for a long time.' Aleobe yawned as he sat up on the small table beside Timothy's bed. 'Sky said it would happen and to let you rest.'

'What happened to me?' Timothy asked as he rubbed his hand down the length of his exposed right arm.

The skin tingled at his touch and deep down he could still feel the resonating warmth. It was, however, nowhere near as intense as it had become when the lion's mouth had spewed out the uncontrollable flames.

'Can you remember being in the training ring?'

Timothy's cheeks flushed as he recalled the events leading up to the unconsciousness swallowing him. He remembered all but begging Sky to let him try to wield the Nosym. His embarrassment was now impossible to contain.

'Yes, I remember trying to conjure the fire,' Timothy sighed. 'I remember losing control of it and then the lion and...'

'The Dark Entity,' Aleobe completed his sentence. 'Yes, you lost all control and vision in your dreams was allowed to manifest.'

'Is that all it was? Just my nightmare and nothing real?'

Aleobe hesitated, and Timothy picked up on it in an instant.

'It's best if Sky explains everything to you.'

'Where is he?'

'He should be back by now. Why don't you get dressed and I'll see where he is.'

Aleobe gave Timothy no chance to reply as he launched off the edge of the table and flew out of the door, leaving Timothy alone. He found his clothes and dressed before leaving the bedroom. Brushing down the fabric, he changed his mind and hung the cape over the end of the bed.

Stepping into the open space that joined all the small subterranean bedrooms, it pleased him to see Sky and Aleobe waiting for him. The two waited at the bottom of the earth staircase.

'How do you feel?' Sky asked as he ended his conversation with Aleobe.

'I've felt better,' Timothy confessed and his rubbed his still-warm right arm.

'It's the residual effect of the eternal flame. Give it a day or two and it will be gone.'

Timothy stopped himself from rubbing his arm and saw Aleobe fly off up the staircase, leaving Sky and him alone in the underground burrow.

'Walk with me?' It was an invitation, and not an instruction, but Timothy was eager to follow either way.

Unlike before, the interior of the tent had been setup like something Timothy had seen in a history book about Roman encampments. A large wooden table dominated most of the space. On it sat an impressive three-dimensional map of all of Mielikuvitus.

Aleobe tiptoed along the ridge of the Torn Mountains that divided the Brightlands and Shadowlands while Sucatraps sat in the room's corner knitting with a yarn of colourful wool.

'Hello,' Timothy greeted the old woman, who raised her attention from the wool for a second to offer him a curt nod.

'Are you quite done, Aleobe?'

The Ecilop stopped mid-step. His blue skin turned two shades darker as he blushed in embarrassment.

'Sorry, I was just,' he stammered, but Sky's raised eyebrow silenced him. 'I'll just go sit over there.'

Aleobe flew from the map and took a seat next to Sucatraps, who offered the little Ecilop a knowing grin.

'I hope now you understand why I was not prepared to let you wield the eternal flame right away?'

'Yes, I didn't realise how difficult it would be.'

That Sky laughed as he walked across to the map table caught Timothy by surprise. As Sky beckoned him to join him at the map, he fought to hide his embarrassment. Turning his attention to the table, Timothy froze mid-step as he saw the landscape moving.

The trees lining the Rainbow River that showed the Mystic Forest wafted in an unfelt breeze. Peering closer, the water of the river churned and the grass, where they were standing, rippled in the wind. Flocks of miniature birds flew in all directions and Timothy realised the table map was a living reflection of Mielikuvitus.

'How is it doing that?' Timothy asked as he looked at the map.

'Look underneath the table.' Sky answered and pointed to the ground beneath the map.

Bending down, Timothy saw that the map was connected to the ground beneath by what looked like the roots of a tree. Thin tendrils stretched from the underside of the table and into the moist earth beneath his feet.

'The map is as much a part of the land as everything else. It lives and breathes as we do.'

It astounded Timothy. Just when he thought he had seen it all, Sky, Sucatraps or Aleobe would show him something new that would fill him with wonder.

'That's amazing.' He gasped in awe at the living map as he stood up.

'I've brought you here to show you something.' Sky began and pointed to the map. 'You see here, the Shadowlands and Shadow Island?'

Timothy followed Sky's hand and saw the dark storm clouds hovering over a lake of black water. In the centre of the wide lake sat a solitary island on which stood an impressive fort. The dark clouds that Timothy had seen from the hillside had changed in shape. Unlike before, when they had appeared nothing more than a mass of hovering storm clouds, it now appeared to be stretching out. The dark cloud looked more like an octopus or spider with many legs stretching out in all directions, spreading out across the lands.

'What was it I saw Sky, when the lion went?' Timothy lifted his attention from the map to look at Sky. 'Aleobe says it was just my nightmare.'

'What do you think it was?'

'I think it was that thing, the Dark Entity. I think it was really him.' Timothy answered, nervousness staining his words. 'Was it?'

Sky pondered for a moment, looking from the legs of the spreading cloud and back to Timothy.

'I think it was both.' He answered.

'What do you mean by both? It was real, or a dream, wasn't it?'

'I don't think it is that simple.' Sky sighed. 'I'm sure you are realising now that a lot of Mielikuvitus' power comes from what you can picture in your mind. It's one consequence of being a Partum Spiritus in your world. The fact your imagination is seen as a curse and something to be tamed and cured.'

'But here we need it. We live because of the power your uniqueness holds.'

'Thank you Aleobe!' Sky cut the Ecilop off. 'Your friend is right. That is why I think what you saw was both real and part of your dreams.'

'I don't understand.'

'You will!' Sky hushed. 'You are connected to the Dark Entity and now he knows you have crossed the realms, he will come for you.'

'The clouds, have they got something to do with it?' Timothy pointed to the spreading storm clouds.

'Yes, I suspect it does. Since you tried to tame the eternal flame, the storm has changed and now, it seems, the Dark Entity is daring to move towards the Brightlands border in search of you.'

Timothy's skin rippled with goose bumps. The thought of the burning eyes searching for him filled him with dread.

'He doesn't know where I am, does he?'

'Not yet,' Sucatraps answered before Sky. 'But it won't take long for him to find you. We must begin your training in earnest. It would seem the fool that allowed you to stumble has inadvertently alerted our enemy to your presence.'

Timothy saw Sucatraps' gaze fix on Sky but the young man remained defiant.

'I saw it best for him to realise the limitations of his mind as it is,' Sky bit back. 'I was unprepared for that level of power and yes Sucatraps I made a misjudgement but it changes nothing.'

'No? It just means we have less time.'

The two continued their back and forth until Timothy silenced them with a loud cough.

'If you're both finished?' Timothy scorned, feigning a confidence he did not feel. 'It's fine. We sit and argue who was right or wrong, but it doesn't change the fact that thing is now looking for me and I'm no nearer to being ready now than I was when I first got here!'

Timothy's word silenced both of them for a moment.

'You're right,' Sky nodded. 'We will venture into the Mystic Forest very soon and use the shadows of the trees to train. We will keep moving, avoiding the wandering gaze of the Dark Entity until we are ready to face him.'

With a nod of approval from Sucatraps they made their plan.

Timothy would begin his training once again.

CHAPTER TWENTY

THE MYSTIC FOREST

T HE SIDE OF THE Rainbow River was their home for the next few days, but even Timothy had noticed the looming clouds in the distance towards the Torn Mountains. On the morning of the third day, he emerged from the tent to find Sucatraps and Sky in deep conversation.

'We need to keep him unseen,' he heard the old woman snap. 'There's too much for him to learn and he is not ready.'

'I agree.' Sky nodded in reply, stroking his colourful beard in thought. 'It is taking a lot to calm his mind, but we are making progress.'

After his exposure to the rage and uncontrollable nature of the eternal flame within the stone circle, Timothy had been subdued. Although he understood Sky's reasoning, it had knocked his confidence. He was more than happy to have followed Sky's lead as he emphasised the need for Timothy to learn to control and quieten his mind.

Somewhat frustrating at first, Timothy had meditated under Sky's tutelage and was doing his best to absorb his surroundings.

He had always been happy in his own company. Timothy's mind had always been a mishmash of train lines pointing in every direction. His uncanny ability to run over more than one train of thought at any one time was both a gift and a hindrance.

Sitting on a cold rock, his eyes closed and focussing on his breathing, his own mind fought against the stillness. His mind flooded with random thoughts and memories, as if constantly trying to distract him.

As the days had passed, the manic nature of his thoughts had slowed and, between the flitting thoughts, he could sense a growing blankness that Sky encouraged him to find. It was still, however, a minimal amount, and he sensed Sky's frustration. Emerging from the tent now, overhearing the conversation of his mentors, he sensed the need for urgency.

Keeping out of sight, Timothy moved around the rear of the tent and looked out to the sky over the Torn Mountains. The heavy, lumbering storm clouds he had seen festering over Shadow Island had spread. Its spider-like fingers of cloud had now reached the valley pass between the mountains and lingered. As Sky had pointed out the morning before, very near the border of the Brightlands.

Each of the wisps of cloud looked and felt familiar as he watched them tumble over and under in the high-altitude winds. It carried the same presence as the smoky apparition in his dreams, the vision he saw of the Dark Entity. Even watching the clouds tumble towards the border, he sensed darkness, and it chilled him to the core.

'I take it you were listening?' Sucatraps coughed as she moved to his side.

Moving in silence, the old woman caught Timothy by surprise and he jumped on the spot when she spoke.

'I tried not to,' Timothy answered in haste and avoided meeting her gaze. 'It didn't seem right, so I came here to look.'

Sucatraps found a large rock and perched herself on it to look out at the silhouette of the Torn Mountains. She had always admired the view. A handful of the jagged peaks climbed high enough to be capped with snow and the mix of browns, greens and white gave the mountain ranges a picturesque and interesting appearance.

'You sense it don't you?' She asked as she looked at the lumbering clouds. 'You know, as I do, that it is searching for you.'

'I haven't dreamt about it as much since I've been here,' Timothy mused as he stood by her side. 'But yes, I feel as if it is out there somewhere.'

'Do you know why it pushed to frighten you away?'

'No.'

'Because it knows that a Partum Spiritus can force it back into hiding.'

'What does it want? I mean, what does it hope to get out of spreading and growing?' It was a question that had niggled him over the last few days.

'The Dark Entity knows the limitations of Mielikuvitus and would seek to spread itself beyond our world.'

Sucatraps' answer was filled with worry. There was something in the motivation of the Dark Entity that unnerved her.

'It wishes to unleash itself into the minds of all those it can. The more minds, the more presence. To survive in the dreams of billions means it will forever have a place, much like the lingering fear it creates that you can never shake.'

'Why? What twisted it to want that?'

Sucatraps played with the crooked walking stick, tapping it against the rock for a moment before she answered.

'Love and loss.' She sighed. 'The Dark Entity once existed alongside us as an ally, but they turned from us when they thought there was nothing left. In hopelessness, they found the shadows and in the shadows that loss festered and grew until the shadow became the darkness and they themselves ceased to be who we knew. They became the Dark Entity.'

'Who were they?'

'Who they were no longer matters,' Sucatraps snapped, a little harsher than she had intended. 'What matters now is the matter that, if left unchecked, the Dark Entity will corrupt our peace and fill the world with hate, anger, suspicion and fear.'

'How can you stop that?'

'I can't,' Sucatraps shook her head. 'But you can!'

The weight of her words hit him with force, much he suspected, as she had intended them to.

'I am trying,' Timothy sighed and dropped his gaze.

'We know you are Timothy. None of us have any doubt of that.' Sucatraps rested a hand on his shoulder to ease his worry. 'What we are asking of you is difficult at the best of times. Your, the Partum before you, were given weeks and months to learn their craft. We face a situation where time is not our friend.'

'Is that because I was wrong to push Sky to let me try to use the Nosym?'

'It was as much your fault as his,' Sucatraps replied, her answer brutal and honest. 'You were not ready and I can see the reason he let you try. None of us knew it would attract the Entity's attention as it did, but we must deal with that now. It has happened and cannot be undone. We should look forward to what we can change and not back to what has already passed.'

Although her words were delivered with the sting of guilt, her wisdom somehow softened the blow. Timothy looked at the old woman and felt an immense amount of respect for her. In her grey eyes, he could sense she had seen a lot in her years.

'What hope do we have if I'm being forced to rush this?'

'More than we would have if you were not here at all!'

Sucatraps was about to continue when a movement caught both their attention. Turning around, they saw Nasser transform from his maroon-coated unicorn into the cloaked man.

'Pardon the intrusion,' he began, his voice sounding regal and formal. 'Sky sent for me and requested I present myself to you.'

'For what purpose?' Sucatraps enquired, as she slid off her perch on the rock.

'There are reports of Hegel-Steffi crossing into the Brightlands north of the Torn Mountains.'

'How many?'

'Hegel-Steffi?' Timothy interrupted. 'Dare I ask what that even means?'

Both Sucatraps and Nasser turned their attention to Timothy. Had the moment not been tainted with a sense of worry, he was sure they would have sniggered at his lack of knowledge.

'Nitram is one of them, or at least one clan of them.'

'The leg-feet-fish, I mean, the fish with legs and feet?' Timothy corrected himself.

Sucatraps did not suppress her smile at Timothy's slip of the tongue.

'Yes, the Leg Feet Fish, as you call him,' she offered him an all-too-familiar disarming smile. 'There are many clans and sadly, most are drawn to the darkness and aligned with the Dark Entity.'

'So what about Nitram?' Timothy pressed.

'Now is not the time,' Nasser cut Timothy's questioning short. 'The scouting parties are still a way from here but we must move to protect you Timothy.'

'Nasser is right; we need to move from here. If the Hegel-Steffi has taken to land, then it has moved from searching to hunting and you are not ready.' Sucatraps turned her attention to Nasser. 'What do you suggest?'

'Sky and I will venture with him into the Mystic Forest. I intend to take him to Conn Uri and continue his training.'

'Before you ask,' Sucatraps had sensed Timothy's curiosity. 'Conn Uri is Nasser's home deep in the Mystic Forest. It will be a good place to continue your training.'

'Will you come?' Timothy asked with haste.

'This is your journey, Timothy, not mine.' She answered, spinning the cane in her hand as she spoke. 'I will try to draw the attention of the Hegel-Steffi towards Partum and give you as much time as I can.'

'That's settled then,' Nasser proclaimed. 'We leave at once for Conn Uri.'

Timothy, in somewhat of a confused daze, followed Nasser and Sucatraps back to the front of the tent where Sky was waiting. Aleobe appeared as the group reconvened at the doors of the tent and offered Sky a knowing nod before turning his attention to Timothy.

It was obvious, to Timothy at least, that there was more going on but he sensed the urgency in them leaving. With little in the way of conversation, he hurried to his subterranean room and gathered up his things.

CHAPTER TWENTY-ONE

NASSER AND CONN URI

N ASSER REMAINED IN HIS human form as they crossed Rainbow River and dismounted the raft onto the far shore. Turning to look back at the tent, Timothy felt a pang of sadness as he watched Sucatraps gathering her belongings together for her journey back to Partum City.

'Will she be all right on her own?' Timothy asked as Sky stepped onto the soft grass.

'She's been through many adventures in her life. I have every faith she will be fine.'

Timothy turned and looked at the tall pastel-leaf trees swaying in the breeze. Up close, the colours of the leaves were even more striking and beautiful.

'We should get moving,' Nasser announced. 'We should reach Conn Uri by sunset.'

Giving the others no time to say anything, Nasser set off towards the tree line. Sky and Timothy gathered their things, now packed in hessian bags, and traipsed across the grass to catch Nasser.

Their journey through the Mystic Forest gave Sky time to help Timothy focus on his training. In a matter of minutes, both Sky and Timothy had lost all sense of direction in the dense forest of pastel trees.

Cracks in the foliage bathed them in patches of light and although the thick canopy of leaves blocked the sun, the leaves were almost transparent. They allowed a surprising amount of light through to the ground.

Following the meandering path through the enchanting forest, Sky helped Timothy to calm his mind. As they climb a long slope upwards, he had mastered a new technique enough to keep his frantic thoughts at bay more than ever.

Reaching the top of the gentle hill, the sun had long passed its highest point and was well on its way towards the distant horizon. Breaching the crest of the hill, Nasser came to a stop and waited for Timothy and Sky to join him.

'We are almost there,' Nasser sighed as he looked out across the impressive view.

The view in front of them was breathtaking, and Timothy stopped mid-step as he reached the hilltop. It was, in fact, not a hill but the long slope of what looked to be a crater that consumed an enormous portion of the Mystic Forest.

From his vantage point, Timothy could see the trees stretching down to the low centre of the crater where an impressive collection of curious structures were gathered.

'Conn Uri?' Timothy gasped.

'Yes,' Nasser beamed with pride. 'The home of my kind.'

The lowest point of the crater was devoid of trees. They had partitioned all the land into vast areas of grazing land.

Even from this distance; Timothy could see herds of unicorns galloping free in the open grassland. In each enormous paddock they had constructed a building of logs, but Timothy could not make out the shape.

'We live free in the paddocks, grazing as we were meant to. At night we live amongst the trees.' Nasser pointed to the trees surrounding the patches of open grass.

Descending from the edge of the crater, Timothy noted the volume of trees grew less the further down they travelled. The colours of the leaves changed in colour from purple to pink and at last blue mixed with patches of pale orange.

'Do the colours mean anything?' Timothy asked as he moved to Nasser's side.

'I beg your pardon?'

'The trees, they've changed colour the nearer we've got to Conn Uri.'

'Legend has it the Mystic Forest grew from the heart of a dying volcano, the orange leaves show where the veins of lava are believed to still flow.' Nasser pointed to a patch of pale-orange trees. 'We have always found the ground rich and tasteful. The first of my kind found that the grass in the crater makes is faster, stronger and our lives linger longer.'

'Enchanted grass?' Timothy scoffed, but hid it as Nasser scowled.

'Remember the differences between our worlds, young Timothy.' Nasser warned and increased his pace, allowing Timothy to drop back to walk with Sky.

It subdued Timothy. The scowl from Nasser had reminded him how out of place he was in Mielikuvitus. For a few moments, he longed for the comfort of his mum's embrace and the cheeky smile of his dad.

Reaching the first massive paddock the dying sun had all but dropped beneath the lip of the crater behind them. Long shadows of the trees were painted across the grass and Nasser guided them to a large structure within the trees.

The herds of infant unicorns that stomped around the lower paddock saw Nasser and galloped across, eager to greet him. As they arrived at the fence, they all transformed into young children. Their faces still equestrian and ears remained as their unicorn ears, along with their shrunken horns protruding from their foreheads.

'Children, children.' Nasser greeted, a warm and caring smile painted on his face. 'Welcome to our guests. This is Sky, who you know, and Timothy a Partum Spiritus.'

All the children's eyes turned to Timothy. He felt self-conscious at their gazes.

'Trainee!' Timothy added, and the children giggled.

After the introductions to the children, Timothy was taken into a vast hall constructed of logs from the forest. Inside was a town. To his surprise, the hall was impossibly large, containing huts and houses as far as Timothy could see.

'We live amongst the trees under the roof of our great hall.' Nasser explained as they walked through the streets between the various wooden buildings. 'You will rest here tonight and resume your tutelage in the morning.'

'I want to see more.' Timothy interjected, awash with fresh curiosity about Conn Uri.

'Not tonight,' Nasser replied, his voice stern. 'We have walked for almost a day and you need to be fresh in the morning. There will be time to see the wonders of Conn Uri but for now, rest.'

Nasser welcomed Timothy into a small wooden hut with a coned roof adorned with leaves of purple and green. With an air of reluctance, Timothy stepped inside and was surprised how overcome he was with tiredness.

'Sleep well Timothy,' Sky offered as he pulled the door closed, leaving Timothy alone. 'Rest and refresh, in the morning we will continue your training.'

Moving to the low bed, Timothy sat on the edge and lay back on the soft sheets. Staring up at the concave interior of the coned roof he felt his eyelids go heavy. Before he could stop himself, Timothy fell into a deep sleep.

***

'You have come to my world against my warning.'

It was the voice of his nightmares, familiar and disturbing as it echoed through the dark cave. Turning on-the-spot Timothy tried to orientate himself but as ever the cave was dark with no sign of light.

'Why have you come?' The Dark Entity asked from the darkness.

Timothy yearned for light. Against his racing heart and rising fear, he took a handful of tentative steps in the darkness.

'There is no point,' the Dark Entity laughed. 'You have nothing here unless I give it to you. This is my world, my island and my home.'

Panic rose and as Timothy felt himself verging on hysteria, he remembered what Sky had told him. Against all his instincts, he closed his eyes and concentrated on his breathing. Doing his best, he drowned out the voice as it continued to question him.

Keeping himself as calm as possible, Timothy tried to ignore the taunts of the Dark Entity and feel a calmness in his heart.

'You are not Partum Spiritus, no matter what that deluded dog tells you.' The Dark Entity mocked.

Timothy fought against the rage at the Dark Entity's scoff and remembered the feeling when the Nosym had burned in his hand. The anger he felt towards the voice bubbled inside him, reminding him of the sensation as the Eternal Flame had exploded from the mouth of the lion.

'They are foolish to shelter you,' the voice mocked. 'I will search you out and destroy everything and everyone that has helped you.'

Acting on instinct, Timothy focussed on the churning sensation and felt it once again as a heat in his arm.

With nothing in his hand, he opened his palm and held it out in front of him. At first nothing happened. The heat beneath his skin was nowhere near as intense as it had been with the Nosym gripped in his palm but he could still feel it.

'You have no power. You are a boy, nothing more than a child in *my* world.'

Fuelled with frustration, Timothy fought to intensify the feeling in his arm until something happened. In the air above the palm of his open hand, a spark ignited in the darkness. A brief burst of light that died in an instant, but it had been there. Opening his eyes, Timothy stared at where the light had burned and concentrated again.

The warmth grew hotter beneath his skin until again a spark appeared, followed by another and then another.

'The fire will not burn for you. My darkness is too powerful.'

'No it isn't.' Timothy answered at last.

No sooner had he spoken than the spark flickered and ignited into a small ball of flame hovering above the skin on the palm of his hand. The ball of fire rotated like a sun and the flames coned upwards away from his hand.

'Less light than a dwindling candle,' the Dark Entity mocked, but his voice betrayed his nervousness as the orb of flame grew and the light spread in the cave.

Timothy stared at the light as it illuminated the floor. For the first time, he saw the charcoal stone beneath his feet. Raising his attention to the ball of fire, Timothy saw the burning red eyes appear in the space beyond the limit of the light.

'It means nothing to me what you can do. Your destiny is to die and mine is to rise. You have crossed into my world now.'

As the eyes closed in on him, Timothy screamed and the ball of fire exploded.

Sitting bolt upright in the bed, Timothy was, as always, drenched in sweat, but for the first time he was not afraid. He didn't notice the faint plume of smoke from his hand as he wiped the sweat from his brow.

CHAPTER TWENTY-TWO

SPARKS AND FLAMES

AFTER THE FIRST NIGHT and curious revision of his recurring dream, Timothy woke with a fresh determination. As he hurried to finish his breakfast, a strange concoction of cereals he dare not even try to guess, he looked around for Sky.

Catching sight of his mentor, he had spooned the last morsel of food into his mouth and launched from the table. A handful of the young unicorn-children were startled by his sudden movements and their horsey ears twitched as they watched Timothy dart between the rows of tables in the large dining hall.

'Sky, I need to talk to you.' Timothy proclaimed as he caught his attention. 'It's important, it's about...'

Sky raised his hand and Timothy skidded to a halt by Sky's side. Having been so focussed on Sky, he had not noticed Nasser by his side and the fact the two of them were deep in conversation. As Sky cast him a warning glance, Timothy realised whatever they were talking about was serious.

Both men exchanged hushed words, their voices quiet on purpose to keep Timothy from hearing what they were saying.

After a handful of shared comments, the two men shook hands and Nasser moved away, leaving Sky and Timothy alone at the edge of the dining hall.

'What was so important you had to interrupt us?'

'Sorry.' Timothy apologised and felt like a chastised child.

'So,' Sky pressed. 'What was it you wanted to tell me?'

As they left the hall, Timothy had recounted his dream to Sky, who took a great deal of interest in what he was saying. Absorbing every word, Timothy followed as Sky moved through the covered town of Conn Uri and out to the wide pastures where the infant unicorns had been galloping when they had arrived.

'Interesting. It seems your mind is allowing you to envision the possibilities of your powers. Believe me, that is a positive sign.'

That was the last Sky discussed the dream as he explained his plan for continuing Timothy's training over the coming days. True to his word, they spent the whole day in the open paddock mastering elements of controlling his thoughts until Timothy was far beyond tired.

Having stopped long enough to wolf down a handful of leaf-wrapped items of food delivered by a golden-haired woman, Timothy's energy was all but spent. Overcome with exhaustion, he dropped to the floor. Sitting on the soft grass, he panted for breath as Sky moved across the paddock and perched himself on the perimeter fence.

'Your dream tells me something about you.' Sky announced as he toyed with his beard.

'Yeah, what's that then?' Timothy blurted as he forced himself to stand up and join Sky on the fence.

'You said it was anger that allowed you to set the spark in your hand?'

'Yes, when the Dark Entity was talking, it made me angry. The madder I got, the more the spark burned.'

'It was not anger,' Sky snapped. 'It will never be anger that calls the eternal flame to you, remember that.'

Sky's sudden change took him aback. Turning around, he looked at the young man and waited for him to explain his meaning.

'It is the emotion that burns. Your mind has been chaotic and confused. You have never been in touch with your emotions unless they are forced upon you to an extreme.'

'I feel things.' Timothy defended. 'I feel things all the time.'

'You forget Timothy, I have watched you grow from baby to an infant, infant to boy and boy to Partum. Your feelings have always caused you confusion, and you have developed an ability to box them away, hide them unless they are needed.'

'I find it hard sometimes,' Timothy sighed. 'I've never felt I needed other people. I understand friends and sharing, but I don't get it.'

'That's because you have allowed yourself to believe you are wrong to feel that. Your way may not be the same as those around you but that does not mean it isn't right for you. A Partum with emotions beyond their control is dangerous. You have been left to discover this yourself and your mind has reacted as it should, it has boxed them away to protect you.'

'But you're saying I need them?'

'I'm saying you need to know about them. The fear and anger you felt in your dream allowed you to harness a spark of the eternal flame, hold it in your hand and hold back the Dark Entity, if only for a moment. By quieting the chaos in your mind, we will find a way for you to tap into those emotions. That will help you fuel the fire.'

Sitting on the fence, they spoke well into the evening, far beyond the sunset. Before either of them had realised, the sun had set, and the sky was once again a blanket of flickering stars. Dropping from the fence, Sky invited Timothy to join him. Having exhausted their conversation, they walked back into the wooden walls of Conn Uri to be greeted with a rowdy party atmosphere.

In a heartbeat, the wariness evaporated from Timothy as the high-spirited music and jovial atmosphere welcomed them. As Nasser approached, he explained the customary celebrations when a Partum Spiritus stayed within their walls.

'Before you say anything,' Nasser interrupted, not giving Timothy the chance to protest. 'You need to stop putting yourself down and doubting your abilities. I have seen what you have been doing and sense a change in you. You are a Partum and the sooner you accept this, the better you will feel.'

Thrusting a flagon into his hand, Nasser returned to the dancing crowds filled with Unicorns and transformed men and women who danced along the streets deep in celebration.

There was to be no more talk of learning or training as both Sky and Timothy drank in the atmosphere of the party. Soon they found themselves surrounded by eager eyes and ears of Unicorns in all forms, throwing questions at them from every direction.

By the time Timothy crept into his small hut, he was once again beyond tired. Dropping onto the bed, he slept until late in the morning. This ritual of sleep followed by training continued for the following six days. Each morning he would wake, eat and meet Sky in the paddock to continue his training.

Sky increased the ferocity of his training, and soon Timothy was encouraged to bring his Nosym with him. As Timothy learned to quiet his mind, Nasser always watched from a vantage point in Conn Uri. It was encouraging to see the young boy's improvements. Over the days, he saw a lot of change in Timothy until he watched with nervousness as Sky handed Timothy the Nosym and took several steps back, giving him the space he needed.

The first time Timothy attempted to conjure the eternal flame, there was no response from the Nosym. No flames emerged from the gaping maw of the roaring lion and Timothy finished that day feeling low and unaccomplished.

The following morning was much the same, and he found no flame within the Nosym. In defiance, he tossed the weapon to the floor and stomped across the open grass to the fence where he kicked it in frustration.

'It is there; somewhere inside you and you know that.' Sky sighed as he moved to stand behind Timothy. 'You just have to believe it.'

'I believe it; I'm just scared.'

'Of what?'

'Of what happened last time? I'm scared it will happen again and I'll not be able to stop it.'

'So what if it does?' Sky laughed. 'At least we will know where we stand.'

Sky offered Timothy the Nosym, and he took it with the briefest hesitation. Moving to the centre of the paddock, Timothy closed his eyes and pushed aside the hopes, fears and expectations clouding his mind. Gripping the Nosym tight in both hands, he allowed the crystal heads to face out to either side of him.

Concentrating on his breathing, as Sky had taught him, he allowed the fog of confusing thoughts to lift before concentrating on the emotions he searched for. After what felt like an age, his mind starting to fight with him, he felt a tingle of warmth beneath his skin.

Excitement threatened to boil over, but Timothy re-centred himself enough to keep the excitement at bay. It felt distant, almost impossible to reach, but it was there. Pressing through the labyrinth of his own thoughts, Timothy found the source and focussed on the sensation.

What started as light warmth soon gave way to heat. As beads of sweat from concentration formed on his forehead, the first spark of fire coughed from the open mouth of the snake.

Keeping his eyes clamped shut, Timothy concentrated and focussed on the rising heat beneath his skin.

Unbeknownst to Timothy, a crowd had formed around the fence of the paddock. A handful of curious infant unicorns had gathered at the fence to watch. As Timothy's face contorted with concentration, Nasser and the other adults soon joined the crowd.

Stood in the centre of the field, they watched as Timothy screwed up his face in concentration. Nasser and Sky held their breaths as they watched the first sparks of flame burst from the open mouths on either end of the Nosym. Sparks gave way to a cascade, and the cascade became a flow.

Unlike before, the flames did not grow beyond control. As the length of fire grew further from the open mouths of the lion and snake, the crowds watched as Timothy fought to control it, shape it and tame it.

Recalling the snake's flame, Timothy used all his strength and concentration to retract the flame back into the Nosym. The flame, fighting against Timothy's will, conceded and retracted into the open mouth of the snake until it disappeared from view. Focussing all his attention on the lion's flame, Timothy dared to open his eyes and look to the dancing fire spurting from the Nosym.

Turning the Nosym over in his hand, he changed his grip and widened his stance until the flame was pointed towards the sky.

It was too long, to his mind, and Timothy once again spoke to the strange sensation in his mind and pictured the fire as the blade of a sword.

At first nothing happened, but Timothy would not give in and focussed even harder on the flame. After a few seconds, the length of flickering fire shortened and the flaming tip changed shape until the fire itself took on the appearance of a burning blade.

Filled with pride, he fought the flame back into the Nosym and dropped to the ground exhausted. It was only then, as a plume of smoke drifted from the lion's mouth, that he realised the crowd. Instead of self-consciousness, Timothy filled with a sense of pride at what he had done.

Chapter Twenty-Three

Midnight Invasion

FOUR MORE DAYS PASSED, and by the time the fourth evening arrived, Timothy was spent. His hands were rough, the fingertips showing signs of blistering where the eternal flame had oozed from the mouth of the lion more than once during his attempts to tame the fire.

Compared to where he had been at the start, he felt an intense level of pride at what he had achieved. Aleobe remained with Sky and observed from the paddock fence as he tamed the flame the best he could.

'You have a long way to go, but you have every right to be proud of yourself.' Sky grinned as Timothy climbed over the paddock fencing.

'Thank you.' Timothy looked at Aleobe, who brimmed with pride.

'We have enough time to hone your skills now. In the morning, we will work on changing the flame from one form to another.'

Sky waited as Timothy secured the Nosym on the belt Nasser had given him that morning.

The belt was intricate in its design, shimmering in the dying light. It looked to be made of woven gold and black cloth. Sitting low on his hips, the belt allowed the Nosym to hang in the right position on his side to make the weapon available to him if it was needed.

'Show me your hands,' Sky offered and inspected Timothy's fingers. 'You're working hard. Soak your hands tonight in water from Rainbow River. It'll help soothe the burns.'

Although Timothy longed to explore the intricacies of Conn Uri's covered town, every night by the time he had washed and eaten, all he wanted to do was sleep. As Timothy washed himself and changed into more comfortable clothing, he admired the black and silver-stitched garments Sucatraps had made him. Already they showed signs of wear, but they were by far the most comfortable clothes he had ever worn.

Hanging them over the bed, he dressed in his night-clothes and slumped onto the bed, aware that Aleobe remained outside of the hut presumably talking with Sky.

'Can I come in?' A young voice asked from outside the door to his hut.

'Yes.' Timothy replied and a young boy walked into the hut carrying a wooden bowl.

163

The young boy looked to be about the same age as Timothy, but he kept his eyes on the bowl as if scared to look at him.

Timothy still found the human-unicorn appearance curious. Whereas Sky and Nasser only bore minimal resemblance to their animal forms, the younger unicorns still had the horse-like ears and smaller horn in the centre of their forehead.

'Master Sky has asked you to be given water from the Rainbow River to heal your hands.'

The unicorn boy placed the bowl on the small table and waited.

'Thank you,' with that, the young unicorn-boy disappeared back through the door, leaving Timothy alone.

Rising from the bed, Timothy picked up the bowl and moved back to sit down. With the bowl secured on the bed between his crossed legs, he slipped his hand into the water. Toying with it, he cupped the clear liquid in his hands and lifted his hands to admire the fluid. To his amazement, Timothy watched as the cascading water from his palms fell and allowed him to see the myriad of colours of the rainbow before returning transparent as it settled in the bowl.

Replacing his hands in the water, Timothy soaked his skin in the water and was surprised to feel his skin tingle. Peering into the bowl, he expected to see bubble drifting from his skin but the water was motionless. Closing his eyes, the relaxation swallowed Timothy and soon fell into a light sleep with his back resting against the wall of the wooden hut and his hands submerged in the bowl.

Although sleep came, it was dreamless, perhaps the first time it had been in as long as he could remember.

Swallowed by the near silence, it was the sudden shout of a distant voice that dragged him back from his slumber some time later in the night.

The voice sounded distant but panicked and Timothy sat bolt upright, sending the bowl of water spilling to the floor. Disorientated from the sudden awakening, he looked around the hut and tried to listen for more voices. Another joined the shout, and then another, until it was undeniable that something was happening outside.

Jumping to his feet, Timothy sprinted to the door and as his hand gripped the wooden handle, the door was thrown open sending him tumbling to the floor.

The sight that greeted him chilled him to the core. A fearsome figure dominated the doorframe with its presence as it moved into the hut. Although familiar with its Aquarian look, the Hegel-Steffi dominating the open doorway was far more menacing and imposing than Nitram. Whereas Nitram had resembled a clown fish, orange and black in his skin, this was something different.

The body of a scarred shark balanced on two legs. Its body was almost in a z-shape with the pointed nose and find crooked over to allow the shark Hegel-Steffi to stare at him with its dead black eyes. The dorsal fin was as deformed, bent at an awkward angle, to stop it from dragging on the floor and where its fins would be were now two muscular arms.

'There you are,' the Hegel-Steffi snarled through rows of razor-sharp teeth.

Filled with panic, Timothy rolled and scrambled across the floor to the belted Nosym that hung from the end of his bed. He had made it halfway before he felt the Hegel-Steffi stamp on the centre of his back, pinning him to the floor. Feeling the heat of the creature's breath on the back of his neck, Timothy writhed on the floor to break free.

Try as he might, Timothy was weighed down by the formidable shark-creature and before he could reach for the Nosym, he felt himself hoisted from the floor. Held by the scruff of his neck, he was dragged out of the door into the street beyond. Emerging from the hut, Timothy saw with dismay that the Hegel-Steffi was not alone. Conn Uri was in a state of panic as waves of shark-like creatures smashed through the wooden structures, sending the residents of the town running in every direction.

Women ran with infants as hut after hut were set ablaze by the enraged Hegel-Steffi. As Timothy watched on in horror, the creature that had dragged him from his hut raised its pointed nose to the wooden roof and released a blood-curdling sound that terrified Timothy.

In an instant, the scores of Hegel-Steffi turned to look in Timothy's direction and the pandemonium seemed to falter. A handful of similar looking creatures joined his captor and circled around him. Their dead eyes and crooked faces resembling sinister smile as they looked down at their prize.

Timothy felt outnumbered as the eyes bore down on him, but he maintained his attempts to break free with no success.

As the Hegel-Steffi gripped his clothes, he felt himself once again dragged along the floor, now flanked and protected by a handful of other shark-like creatures.

'Release him!' Sky's familiar voice demanded, and Timothy felt the grip on his neck released in response.

Sky powered down on the squad of Hegel-Steffi and Timothy was relieved as Nasser joined him. Laid prone on the floor, covered with dirt, Timothy watched as his mentor and guide set about freeing him from his sudden captivity.

Sky moved with impressive speed, fighting off the Hegel-Steffi as he moved in almost perfect time with Nasser's attacks. Unlike Sky, Nasser transformed from unicorn and back to his semi-human appearance as he fought the menacing creatures.

Leaping over, under, through and around, Timothy was surprised by Nasser's agility as he pushed back and powered down on the gathered captors. Several of them were armed with jagged weapons but were promptly disarmed by Sky and Nasser, leaving them to fight only with their bare hands.

As their numbers dwindled, the lead Hegel-Steffi once again raised his head to the sky and released a similar sound that echoed all around. Without exception, every Hegel-Steffi reacted to the call and ceased their activity. Before Nasser or Sky could do anything more, all the creatures turned and fled from inside the shrouded unicorn town.

Cheers erupted from the residents as the Hegel-Steffi made good their escape, leaving a smouldering mess behind them. Looking around with great dismay and sadness, Nasser felt a swell of pride as the terrified residents of his town set about dousing the flames and helping those that had been attacked in the midnight raid.

'What was that about?' Timothy asked as he stood from the floor.

Nasser snapped his head around, still enraged by the attack, but softened his expression to answer Timothy as best he could.

'The Dark Entity has been more daring than we would have expected.' Nasser growled. 'They were here for you!'

There was accusation and frustration in his voice, and Timothy felt guilt at Nasser's words.

'Master Nasser, Master Nasser...'

A frantic voice bellowed as the same young unicorn that had delivered Timothy the bowl of water came running along the street.

'What is it?'

'They've taken the children,' the young unicorn panted as he skidded to a halt between Nasser and Sky.

'What do you mean?'

'The Hegel, they took the children.'

Nasser's eyes went wide and as he sprinted off across Conn Uri. As he moved with haste, both Sky and Timothy fell into step behind him.

They reached the burning nursery as the last of the flames were doused by a handful of frantic unicorns. An old woman with a head of bright-orange hair staggered across to them. Her face was bruised and dusted with black from the smoke of the fire.

'What happened?' Nasser boomed as he looked at the smouldering wreckage.

'They came and took fifteen of my children. I couldn't stop them.' The old woman wept.

As Nasser comforted her, resting her head against his chest, he turned his attention to Sky.

'Ready or not, I will leave for Shadow Island in the morning. Your protégé will either join us or I will face the Entity alone and rescue my children.'

Releasing the older unicorn woman, Nasser stalked off, leaving Sky and Timothy alone to soak in the destruction left behind by the Hegel-Steffi.

'I'll go with him!' Timothy declared as he looked at the forlorn woman.

Sky did not offer an argument, there was little he could or would say to dissuade Timothy, even if he had wanted to.

CHAPTER TWENTY-FOUR

CROSSING TO THE SHADOWLANDS

D AWN BROKE, AND THE mood of Conn Uri was sombre and subdued. Timothy dressed in silence and emerged from the hut to find Nasser and Sky waiting for him. A half-dozen other unicorn-men were gathered off behind Nasser and appeared to be guards to their venture.

'We leave at once.' Nasser hushed. 'We eat on the move. It will be three days to the Shadowlands and I would waste no more time in leaving.'

Holding out a hessian bag, Timothy took it and checked the contents. They had stuffed parcels of food into the bag and it carried a substantial weight. As he was about to protest at the weight, he caught Sky's eye, who offered him a warning shake of his head to stop him in his tracks.

Choosing to keep his complaint to himself, Timothy shouldered the bag and adjusted the cape over his right shoulder. As Sky handed him a parcel of food, he started to eat as the group moved through Conn Uri and started their journey towards the Shadowlands.

The mood was sombre for the first day, and they moved at a laboured pace to accommodate Timothy. It was clear, as the sun passed its highest point in the midday sky, the pace was frustrating Nasser. Calling two of the accompanying troops to him, Nasser gave hushed instructions and Timothy watched as they ran ahead of the group. Timothy watched as they transformed into their unicorn-form and galloped off into the distance.

'They will set off ahead and secure us a camp for the night.' Nasser explained, not breaking his attention from his galloping companions as they cantered away. 'It will give us something to work towards, as I expect to make the Torn Valley before nightfall.'

It was Sky who offered a protest this time as he moved to Nasser's side.

'That is some distance to cover in a day,' Sky pleaded. 'Perhaps we could consider a destination a little nearer?'

'I will not leave my children in the hands of the Entity any longer than I have to.' Nasser snapped in reply and stalked ahead of the group to increase his distance from Timothy and Sky.

'I know he's mad at me.' Timothy sighed as he walked by Sky's side.

'He's not mad at you,' Sky corrected. 'We all know this isn't because of you, but you have to understand the concern he has for his people.'

'I feel it's my fault.'

'Don't!' Sky snapped. 'Your being here is a risk. A risk that Nasser, Sucatraps and all the Elders knew of and accepted. You are here to protect us. As terrible as this is, it is not for you to accept responsibility.'

'Doesn't feel that way.' Timothy scoffed and dragged his feet as he walked, very much showing his age for a moment.

'Don't let it win. The Dark Entity feeds on that sort of thinking.'

They spent the rest of the day in silence. Timothy admired the changing scenery around them as they neared the towering Torn Mountains. The landscape had started off as dense forestry but soon opened into plains of rock and grass. Later in the day, they reached the foot of the mountains as dusk settled.

Aleobe remained with him, perched on Timothy's shoulder, watching the world as they walked. Timothy felt comfort in having his friend by his side, even if they walked in silence.

'We rest there for the night.' Nasser announced as he pointed across the dark open land to a flickering fire in the distance where his consort waited. 'Eat, sleep and when the sun rises, we move again.'

Nasser shared no more words with Timothy that night and for the first time since arriving in Mielikuvitus, Timothy felt out of place. Wrapped in a thick blanket, his head resting on the hessian bag, Timothy stared up at the stars and waited for sleep to take him.

Morning broke and before the sun had even crested above the horizon, they were on the move again. Nasser despatched the same two unicorns from their escort ahead of them. As the feathery clouds were bathed in the rich red and orange of the dawn sun, they began their journey to the border.

As the morning crept towards afternoon, Sky moved to Timothy's side and produced a piece of folded fabric from his inside pocket. Unfolding the vast sheeting, Timothy saw the same map embroidered on the cloth that he had seen on the living map at Rainbow River. Sky explained their route and pointed to the valley between the two ranges of the Torn Mountains.

'The border between the Shadowlands and the Brightlands is just here.' Sky explained and pointed to the furthest edge of the mountains on the map. 'If you look ahead of you, you will see where the land changes.'

As Timothy raised his gaze, he could indeed make out the difference in the topography and colouring of the land. As the jagged mountains of the valley flanked them on either side, he could see the land beyond the furthest side, darker and tainted with shadow and a hue of grey.

The storm clouds still raged in the sky ahead of them and a tentacle of black cloud stretched above them, inching deeper into the Brightlands from where they had come. As the rumble of thunder increased, they inched closer to the border. Once they reached the physical divide between the two regions, Nasser brought the caravan to a halt.

'We will break for food,' he announced and turned his attention to Timothy. 'A word if I may?'

Timothy obliged and under the watchful eyes of Sky, Nasser wandered to an outcrop of rock and hoisted Timothy up to look out across the Shadowlands.

'This will be the first time in many years that anyone has crossed, willingly, into the Shadowlands.' Nasser began. 'I must apologise for my abruptness these past days. I do not blame you for what has happened, but I am sure you appreciate the concern for my children?'

'I do,' Timothy sighed. 'And you may not blame me, but I do.'

'Well, you shouldn't.' He caught him by surprise.

Nasser wrapped his arm around Timothy's shoulder and did his best to mend the gap that had built between them since leaving Conn Uri. Timothy felt relief as Nasser comforted him and he felt the tears well in his eyes as he looked out across the barren and imposing landscape.

Compared to the Brightlands, the Shadowlands were a desolate place. The ground was tainted with an earthy, ashen colour and the heavy sky blocked out the sunlight from the sky. The Shadowlands, as he could see, were as imposing and dark as they had led him to believe. What little light there was that crept through the cracks in the lumbering clouds was intermittent and quickly obscured.

'The Black Lake is another day from here and who knows what awaits us on the Shadow Island?'

Nasser left Timothy alone on the outcrop of rock to stare into the foreboding landscape ahead of him. Timothy ate little and watched the dancing streaks of lightning as they zigzagged and cracked in every direction across the sky.

When the time came for them to move, Timothy's mood had dropped. As he passed over the physical divisions that marked the border between the two lands, he felt a chill against his skin.

Although they had made it this far unhindered and unopposed by the Hegel-Steffi or anything else that crept amongst the shadows, Timothy still felt as if something in the darkness ahead of them was searching for him.

By the time they made camp amongst a copse of leafless trees, Timothy could not shake the feeling they were being watched. With the fire extinguished, his sense of unease had spread to everyone in the group, and that night, everyone jumped at the slightest sound of movement beyond the limit of what they could see.

Unable to see the sun or guess what time they were at, after hours of troubled sleep, it was decided they would muster their things and continue deeper into the Shadowlands. With the group remaining together, huddled close to one another, Timothy felt his hand caressing the Nosym that hung by his side.

By mid-afternoon they could see the Black Lake in the distance, the black glassy surface of the water reflecting the sporadic sparks of lightning.

CHAPTER TWENTY-FIVE

THE SHOCKTOPUS

T HE FACELESS CLIFFS OFFERED the Black Lake protection. A sheer drop of jagged rocks led down to the still water far below. Having navigated to the top of the cliffs, Timothy felt a wave of vertigo as he inched to the crumbling edge and looked down.

Having spent enough time in the Shadowlands, Timothy's eyes had adjusted and he could see more detail of the world around him than he had expected. Peering over the edge, the water shimmered but there as something else that stole Timothy's attention.

Sat in the centre of the Black Lake was a solitary island. Silhouetted against the lake, Timothy could make out enough detail to see the angular fort dominating most of the island. Shadow Island looked at odds with the surrounding water.

Somewhat like an irregular droplet of water splashing up with a handful of precarious rocks surrounding the main island.

'What's that?' Timothy hushed as he crouched on the cliff edge.

Pointing out across the Black Lake, Timothy could see a terrifying figure floating above Shadow Island. Silhouetted against the stormy clouds was something Timothy could not explain.

'The Dark Entity has grown more powerful than I imagined.' Sky sighed as he followed Timothy's gaze to the terrifying sight.

Suspended in the air, moving majestically, as if suspended under water was an enormous octopus. Larger than the island itself, the ink-black octopus moved in slow motion. Its enormous tentacles circled above the rocks, as if protecting the island beneath it.

Even at their distance, viewing from the cliffs, the octopus was a terrifying sight. As the creature rotated in the air its lifeless eyes scanned its surroundings, searching for anyone that dared to approach.

'That is a Shocktopus.' Sky explained. 'That is the source of the storm. It gives life to the expanding darkness. That thing is the guardian of Shadow Island.'

Tracing the outline of the Shocktopus with his eyes, Timothy could just make out the billowing clouds rising into the sky from the top of the Shocktopus' head. The clouds cascaded upwards with ferocity and looked to Timothy like a volcanic eruption. As he scanned the sky, bolts of lightning erupted from the crown of the Shocktopus' head. The electricity disappeared into the storm clouds, spreading far and wide across the Shad-owlands.

'That gives us a whole new problem to contend with.' Nasser groaned and sat on the edge with his legs dangling over the cliffs.

'Why?'

'The Shocktopus feeds on fear. She senses it and hones towards it. The moment we touch the Black Lake she will know we are here.'

'Getting down to the lake will be difficult enough.' Sky pondered as he tossed a rock over the edge of the cliffs.

Far below, as the lake swallowed the splash of the rock, the Shocktopus snatched its attention to the slightest movement and glared at the water beneath them. As the Shocktopus' attention bore down on the movement in the still water, Timothy could make out where the Shocktopus was directing its attention as the water appeared lighter, its eyes acting like spotlights in the dark.

'What do you suggest?' Nasser pressed as the Shocktopus' attention returned to Shadow Island in the centre of the lake.

'We will rest and come up with something.' Sky answered and stepped back from the cliffs.

Observing the movements of the Shocktopus, Timothy allowed Nasser and Sky to reconvene out of view of the cliffs and the wandering eyes. Timothy remained transfixed by the curious sight ahead of him. Never in his wildest dreams would he have imagined the sights he had seen so far in Mielikuvitus. His own imagination and the worlds he had always escaped into when life became too much for him paled when compared to what he had seen so far. He knew, deep down, he had only scratched the surface.

Looking across the Black Lake, Timothy felt the weight of what was ahead of him. Less than two weeks had passed since he had crossed into Mielikuvitus and so much had changed. Timothy felt like a different person, but still the uncertainty in his capability clawed at him. To Timothy, it seemed impossible that he would even consider what he had done as possible.

Sat on the coarse floor, Timothy unhooked the Nosym from his side and laid it on his lap. Admiring the weapon, it was an amazing artefact to behold. Picking it up, he studied the carved crystal heads of both the lion and the snake and allowed his mind to wander. He remained there alone, swallowed by his thoughts for some time, before Sky approached from his meeting with Nasser.

'You will need everything I've taught you so far.' Sky announced, making him jump.

'What is on that island?'

'You already know the answer, Timothy,' Sky mused and took a seat on the floor by his side. 'Nobody but you can prepare you for what you will face. Nasser, Sucatraps and I can only give you the tools to face it. The rest, my friend, is up to you.'

'You said the Dark Entity was more powerful than you had thought. What did you mean?' Timothy did not hide the trepidation in his voice.

'The Shocktopus is a creature that has lived in the Black Lake for centuries, little more than a myth in recent history.' Sky turned his attention to the creature in the sky. 'The fact the Dark Entity has raised it from the depths tells me it has become more connected with the darkness than I would have believed.'

'Is he going to be there?'

'The fact the Shocktopus is there would tell me yes.'

'And those shark-people things?'

'The Hegel-Steffi who invaded Conn Uri? Yes, they will be there. If we make it onto Shadow Island, we will face scores of them. But that is not for you to concern yourself with.'

'How is that?' Timothy snapped.

'Because Nasser and I have discussed a plan with the others. We will draw the attention of the Hegel-Steffi and you will seek the Dark Entity and face it.'

'Alone?'

'There is no other way.' Sky attempted to ease Timothy's worry. 'With the Hegel-Steffi distracted, the Entity will be alone. There will be no escape and you have everything you need to face him.'

'I'll need you.' Timothy pleaded.

'You have never needed me. You are the one to master the flame and your Nosym. All I've tried to do is show you how. The rest has always been down to you.'

'What about others from Conn Uri or Partum? Can't they come to help?'

181

'It's taken us days to come this far. To send messengers back and gather the required numbers would take too long.

Timothy was unconvinced. It was obvious by his face.

'There are hardly any of us.'

'The fewer, the better in this case. If we leave it any longer, we risk the Dark Entity growing beyond something we can manage without an army.'

The two of them fell silent and stared out across the Black lake and towards the Shocktopus. Whatever plans Nasser and Sky had mustered for crossing the Black Lake had not been shared with Timothy. For the moment, that was irrelevant. Weighing up what was about to happen, the risks he was taking and the expectation that weighed on his shoulders, Timothy could not help but feel the rising shadow of concern building in the pit of his stomach.

Toying with the Nosym, rolling it around in his hands, Timothy did the only thing that felt right. Closing his eyes, he tried his best to follow Sky's words and calm his racing mind against the tidal wave of emotions that threatened to bubble over at any moment. Finding the flickering flame of the candle in his mind, Timothy pushed aside the shadow of fear. In the air, all he could hear was the rumble and crack of the approaching storm.

'You are strong enough you know,' Aleobe comforted as he inched towards the edge of the cliff with trepidation. 'I knew from the moment I was asked to guard you, you would be something in my world.'

'I don't feel like something,' Timothy confessed. 'Right now I feel like a boy out of his depth in a place he doesn't belong.'

'Sky was wrong about one thing, though.' Aleobe declared, as he turned and launched himself backwards over the cliff. 'You won't be alone because I will be with you.'

Timothy could not help but crack a smile as his old friend rolled and tumbled through the air like an excited insect. The time was fast approaching that he would face the nightmare that had haunted him for years. Deep down, Timothy hoped it would bring finality and free him from the darkness if he ever returned home.

If he returned home.

CHAPTER TWENTY-SIX

CROSSING THE BLACK LAKE

CROSSING THE TOP OF the Faceless Cliffs, the caravan of Timothy and his companions searched for a way down to the water below. The sheer face of the rocks look impossible to scale and for many hours they followed the line of the cliffs until they felt the land starting to descend.

'Another hour and I can see a shore.' One of the scouting party that moved a little way ahead of them announced.

The scouting unicorn had been right. A short while later, Timothy scrambled down a rocky bank and found himself stood on a beach of coarse black sand. Aleobe dropped to the ground and dragged his hand through the sand. Lifting a handful to his face, he inspected it curiously. As the little Ecilop sniffed the sand, he wrinkled his nose in disgust.

'Smells awful,' he choked and brushed the sand from his hands. 'So Sky, how do you intend on crossing that?'

Aleobe pointed out across the vast expanse of churning water that was the Black Lake. The crests of waves stretched as far as they could see and still, in the distance, the Shocktopus swam in the air above Shadow Island.

'Rest, let me sort that.' Sky announced and stalked off along the beach, away from them.

Left alone, Aleobe and Timothy moved to the water's edge and watched the jet-black water lapping against the shoreline. There was no sound in the air. The Black Lake was eerie and silent as the pair stood looking out at Shadow Island.

'We should eat.' Aleobe offered after some time of staring at the Shocktopus. He had sensed the rising tension in Timothy as they watched. 'Sky won't be long and I expect he will want to move as soon as he is ready.'

Not questioning how they would make the voyage across the lake, Timothy moved back from the waves and joined Aleobe. They sat with the gathered scout unicorns that had journeyed this far with them. Between them, they talked and ate. The hushed conversations between the accompanying scouts were too hard for Timothy to hear.

'We leave at once.' Sky announced from behind them.

Timothy felt relief as the awkward disconnect between himself, Aleobe, and the unicorn men had become unbearable.

'How are we going to?' Timothy stopped short as he saw four rafts bobbing on the water's edge.

'I may not be Partum, but I have my own tricks still!' Sky laughed and pointed to the four rafts. 'You, Nasser and I will take one and our companions will divide amongst the others.'

As he gave the instruction, those huddled near Timothy burst into movement.

In no time at all, they divided the party between the four rafts and launched into the wide expanse of the Black Lake.

The sounds of the waves lapping against the shore soon faded, and Timothy felt the silence wrapping around them. The air was still and unmoving; although there were waves across the water's surface, there was no accompanying breeze. The Black lake, to Timothy, felt a dead and lifeless place.

As Nasser and Sky paddled either side of the raft, Timothy moved to the front and looked into the black-glass surface of the lake. He could see nothing beneath them. There was no light and in the darkness, he could hardly make out his own reflection in the water.

'Be careful,' Nasser hushed from behind him. 'You don't know what lurks beneath the surface.'

'Like what?'

As if to answer his question, Timothy saw the fin of a shark breach the surface of the water ahead of them. In response, both Nasser and Sky lifted their oars from the water and let out a whistle to alert the other rafts.

Tension filled the air as the fin was joined by five others that circled ahead of them in the water. Large and imposing, all eyes watched as the fins glided through the water in all directions around the four floating rafts.

'Hegel-Steffi.' Sky murmured in Timothy's ear as they watched. 'They can't see us, but I would rather us not alert the Dark Entity any earlier than necessary. They'll move on soon enough if we remain silent.'

True to Sky's prediction, the fins disappeared back beneath the surface and after a few moments of waiting; the oars returned into the water. Once again, the rafts glided across the Black Lake once again.

Inching closer to Shadow Island, Timothy could see the terrifying size of the Shocktopus suspended in the air above the island. He had seen nothing so terrifying or enormous in all his life. As they neared the monster, he tried to fathom a comparison to its size in the real world, but it was beyond comprehension.

'Hold your nerve Timothy.' Nasser instructed as he paddled in the water. 'The nearer we get, the more the Shocktopus will sense your fear.'

'It's kind of hard.' Timothy replied sarcastically, masking his fear.

The nearer they moved to the Shocktopus, the sound of its tentacles wafting through the air became more noticeable. Although the monster moved as if held underwater, the massive tentacles disturbed the air. Although the bulbous head of the Shocktopus touched the clouds, the snake-like tentacles moved just above the water's surface as it swam in the air, protecting the island beneath it.

The pace of paddling decreased as the four rafts bobbed closer to where the tentacle tips brushed against the churning lake. Timothy watched as one tentacle moved through the air in front of the raft and he could make out every detail of its slimy skin and suction-cupped flesh.

It was a disturbing sight to behold and Timothy's skin goose bumped as he watched the tentacle float back and forth in front of them.

'We need to time it right to remain unseen.' Sky announced and started watching the rhythmic pattern of the Shocktopus.

Adjusting the position of the raft, Timothy saw the others doing the same. Together, they inched closer to where the crooked tip of the tentacle moved over the water. Perched on the front of the raft, Timothy felt the spray of water as the tentacle wafted past within touching distance of him.

Heart racing, pounding like a drum in his ears, Timothy watched the tentacle fly off to the left and then drift back towards them. As it passed in front of the raft again, both Nassar and Sky dragged their oars through the water, propelling the raft forward.

Timothy was transfixed on the wafting tentacle and watched as it reached the height of its upward movement before it started to fly back towards them.

'It's coming back.' He stammered, but neither Nasser nor Sky acknowledged him.

As the raft dragged forward, the tentacle swooped towards them and Timothy was convinced it would hit them. Closing his eyes, he waited for inevitable impact as the tentacle crashed into the wooden raft and sent them flying into the churning waters.

The crash never came and when he dared to open his eyes, Timothy felt relief as he saw the tentacle swoop past the back of the raft. They had, by some miracle, made it.

The third raft, however, was not so lucky. As it passed, the most dangerous point on the edge of the tentacle collided with the back corner of the raft, sending it spinning in the water. The attention of the Shocktopus was on them in an instant. It bathed both the raft and the surrounding water in the dim light as the eyes of the creature focussed on it.

Timothy rose and watched in horror as the Shocktopus tentacles stopped moving. The air filled with the sound of gathering electricity, that sickening sound before lightning strikes. Timothy felt his hair prickle as the air became charged with static. The Shocktopus raised the tentacle that had collided with the raft high into the air and Timothy watched as bolts of electricity zipped and crackled between the suction-cups on its flesh.

Unable to say or do anything, Timothy watched as the sparks zigzagged along the length of the tentacle. After a brief pause the Shocktopus slammed the charged appendage on top of the raft. The three unicorns had no time to react as the electrified tentacle smashed into them. The water exploded, cascading water in every direction and soaking the occupants of the remaining three rafts.

Shielding himself from the water, Timothy wiped his face clear and looked on as the tentacle rose back from the water. Where it had impacted with the raft, there was nothing left, save for the wreckage of the wood that had been obliterated by the attack. As the eyes of the Shocktopus scanned the water around the destroyed raft, everyone remained silent.

When the Shocktopus had searched enough and found nothing to focus its attention on the mood between the survivors was dampened. Having searched for any sign of survivors from the annihilated raft, those that remained resumed their journey towards Shadow Island.

As the island grew larger in front of them, Timothy could not shake the sickening feeling that the odds were stacked even more against them.

CHAPTER TWENTY-SEVEN

SHADOW ISLAND

WAVES CRASHED AGAINST THE rough rocks of Shadow Island. Each of the rafts fought against the current and turbulence as it dragged and pushed them closer into danger. Circling to the north of the island Sky, his beard soaked with the ocean spray, identified the mouth of a wide cave at the base of the island.

'There.' He bellowed over the sound of water smashing into the rocks.

Fighting with all their strength, those that powered the rafts moved them closer to the opening and fought to keep on course as the waves grew rougher. With the raft being tossed from side-to-side Aleobe had taken to flight and moved ahead of them to scout their landing. Timothy, on the other hand, had found enough loose rope to anchor himself to the surface of the raft.

Aleobe fluttered back and spoke with Sky as they fought against the current.

'The water in the cave is shallow and there's a path leading up.'

'Good!' Sky bellowed over the crashing waves.

Holding on for dear life, Timothy closed his eyes and did not open them until they had made it through the mouth of the cave. The sound of the crashing waves abated as the cave swallowed them. They paddled on until Sky and Nasser's oars scraped across the shallow bottom of the cave's pool.

The slow rhythm of dripping water was familiar and for a moment, Timothy feared he was in his nightmare. Forcing his eyes open, he felt relief to find his companions dismounting the raft and dropping into the waist-high water.

'We should move,' Nasser declared as he pulled his bag from the raft and slung it over his shoulder. 'The Shocktopus has already cost us three of my people. It stacks the odds against us and we risk losing the element of surprise.'

Since the Shocktopus had destroyed the raft, Nasser's intensity had doubled. He had barely uttered a word. Timothy had avoided his defiant glare as they moved beneath the Shocktopus and closed the distance to Shadow Island. Now they had made it into the cavern, Nasser's anger was tangible.

Timothy watched as Nasser rejoined the rest of the unicorn-men that had come with them and began devising their plans. As Timothy shuffled across the raft, Sky offered him a hand as he dropped into the cold water. Being shorter than the adults, Timothy was self-conscious as the water reached well above his waist, but he did his best not to show it.

'The fort is above us.' Sky explained as they waded back towards the mouth of the cave. 'Aleobe says there is a narrow path leading from the opening and up the rocks to the island; we take that and see what we do from there.'

It worried Timothy as they moved back towards the opening of the cave as the water inched higher up his body. By the time he reached the mouth of the cave, the water had reached his chin. He was grateful when Sky reached down and hoisted him out of the water and onto the narrow path etched in the rock face.

Nasser still paid him no attention as they began their ascent in silence. Once again, Aleobe, having found his niche, flew ahead of them and scouted the path all the way to the top. With nothing to report, the group climbed the length of the path and he met them at the top. Timothy was not a fan of the path as it was only wide enough for a single file and more than once, he felt the stones crumbling beneath his feet.

Staring straight ahead, Timothy was shaking as the path narrowed even more as they neared the top of the path. Feeling relief as they reached the top, Timothy could not move fast enough to get away from the perilous edge of the rocks.

'Shadow Island Fort.' Sky announced and pointed at their destination.

Timothy stepped in front of the group and took in the impressive sight in front of him. Words escaped him as he looked at the angular structure protruding from the island. The walls were made of a blue crystal laced with intricate veins of pale stone. Unbeknownst to Timothy, they had constructed the whole fort from sodalite crystal. Fires burned all around the fort, casting dancing light in all directions and illuminating the shimmering blue stone that made-up the imposing fortified building.

The Shocktopus remained poised high above them, but the light from the fort stole too much to allow Timothy to see the underside of the creature in the sky. The fort was made up of a series of outer walls that contained within them a tall main building. Everything had been carved into neat lines, squared and angular, the sodalite box building in the centre of the fort climbed skyward some distance.

'We need to find a way in.' Nasser interrupted as he pushed past Sky and started making his way to the fort.

Not daring to intervene, Timothy fell into position behind Nasser and his companions as they stalked across the barren landscape towards the fort. They walked for some time before the imposing walls towered high in front of them.

They had made it to the wall unseen and, to his surprise, Timothy had seen no sign of guards on the outer wall. It occurred to him, as they stood staring up at the wall, there would be no need for guards. After all, the terrifying Shocktopus protected the island from most who would dare to chart the Black Lake.

Once again, Aleobe acted as a scout and zipped along the length of the wall in front of them. He had been gone for some time and Timothy had worried when the small Ecilop returned gasping for breath.

'What is it?' Nasser snapped as Aleobe landed on Timothy's shoulder to catch his breath.

'Hegel-Steffi,' Aleobe choked. 'Hundreds of them, marching through the gates.'

'Were you seen?'

'No.'

'Good.' Nasser barked as he turned to move along the wall.

'There's more.' Aleobe announced and Nasser turned to face him, his face contorted in a scowl. 'Your infants, those taken from Conn Uri.'

'What of them?'

'They were in cages being taken into the fort.'

'How many?'

'I don't know, I saw at least six or seven but I only saw the end of the marching Hegel-Steffi.'

Nasser growled, his face betraying his intense anger.

'We need to move now.' He turned to look at Sky. 'Whatever you have planned for Timothy, get on with it. I won't leave my children to suffer at the hands of those monsters any longer than necessary.'

'We should wait.' Sky argued, but Nasser towered over him.

'I will not wait! Do what you want, I'm going.'

Nasser turned his back on Sky, who stood rooted to the spot torn.

'Nasser!' Timothy shouted, and all eyes turned to him. 'I can't even say I understand what you're going through.'

'You're too young to understand.'

'Whatever Sky has planned, he needs us to work together. We have come too far now to risk it falling apart.'

'Our reasons for being here are different.'

'Are they?' Timothy snapped, his confidence and demeanour catching everyone by surprise. 'What is stopping this from happening again in days or weeks? The Hegel-Steffi crossing the border and taking your children again?'

'Nothing.'

'Wrong!' Timothy replied and pulled the Nosym from his belt. 'If we act independently, you're right, there is nothing that will stop them. If we work together, if you let Sky take me to where I need to face the Dark Entity, then maybe, just maybe, there will be something to stop it.'

Nasser moved to stand in front of Timothy, the scowl still etched on his face. Staring down at Timothy, he weighed up what the boy was saying to him for a moment.

'I've stood in the shadows and watched you grow with Sky's help.' Nasser began and Timothy swelled with pride. 'But you said it yourself. You are a young boy and the task ahead of us is one you are not ready for.'

Timothy felt deflated as the words hit him like a brick wall. What pride he had felt evaporated in an instant as Nasser softened a little and placed his hand on Timothy's shoulder.

'If you were older, if we had more time, then maybe you would be right.' Nasser sighed. 'You just aren't ready.'

Squeezing Timothy's shoulder, Nasser turned and moved to walk away. Stunned into silence, Timothy had no answer for the unicorn. Before Nasser could take a step, Sky pressed forward and took hold of his arm, stopping him mid-step.

'You trusted me when I brought Timothy to your home.' Sky said. 'Trust me now when I say we can finish what we started.'

'I would have believed you if we had given you more time.'

Never turning to face Sky, Nasser pulled his arm free and stormed away.

What happened next caught everyone by surprise. Using every element of what Sky had taught him, harnessing and controlling the raging eternal flame, Timothy called forth the fire from both ends of his Nosym. Taming the fire, controlling and shaping it, Timothy created the same bow Sky had shown him. Drawing his fingers across the thin string, he drew it back and loosed an arrow of flame through the air.

The burning arrow flew past the side of Nasser's head and buried itself in the sodalite wall a short way in front of him. The burning air stopped him dead in his tracks, and Nasser turned to glare at Timothy.

'We have a chance to stop this getting any worse. Let me try.'

Allowing the flame to return into the gaping mouths of the lion and snake, Timothy's face was stern and determined. Nasser mulled over what had happened and, with a great reluctance, nodded, accepting Timothy's offer.

Chapter Twenty-Eight

Live In The Fort

A long the outer walls of the fort, they saw and heard nothing to show the imposing structure was home to anyone. That all changed as the group rounded the final corner before the open gates and saw a hive of activity.

Scores of Hegel-Steffi marched through the vast onyx gates. They moved in neat files, marching their preposterous legs as they moved about their business. Chancing a peek around the corner, Timothy felt uneasy at the sheer number of them around the gates.

'There are loads of them.' He gasped and returned to the cover of the perimeter wall.

'That's not your concern.' Sky announced and turned to look around them.

There was enough cover for his plan and although their numbers had dwindled since the sinking of the raft, there was still hope they would succeed. After Timothy's defiant demand for Nasser to trust him, Sky and the unicorn had debated enough a plan of what could be done. It was now time to put that plan into action.

'Timothy,' Sky began. 'You, Nasser and Aleobe will infiltrate the fort while myself and the rest of Nasser's unicorns will draw out as many of the Hegel-Steffi as we can.'

'They'll overpower you in seconds.' Timothy protested, but Sky silenced him with a raised hand.

'I have my tricks Timothy, there will be enough of us to convince them they are under threat.' Sky explained. 'You will wait here and when the time is right, the three of you will infiltrate the fort and set about your missions.'

'I will help Nasser and then seek the Dark Entity.'

'That isn't the plan.' Nasser interrupted. 'Once inside, you must take advantage of the distractions. We create and find the Blue Hall and face the Entity.'

'But the children.' Timothy tried to argue.

'I will find them and free them. It is the only way we have a chance of success.'

Although it pained Timothy, he knew they were right. Shifting the cape from his right side, he ensured the Nosym was hooked to his belt and pulled the hood up over his head for the first time.

'It has been my pleasure to show you my world, Timothy Scott.' Sky offered as he held out his hand to Timothy.

Timothy felt a lump in his throat as he took Sky's hand and he shook it. Grasping Timothy's hand in both of his, Sky pulled him to him and embraced Timothy in a tight hug.

'You've grown so much in such a short space of time; imagine what we could have achieved with months instead of weeks.' Sky muttered as he slapped Timothy's back.

'Thank you for everything.'

'You are stronger than you think you are. Don't let the fact you are different hold you back. That curse in your world is a gift in ours.'

Sky released Timothy, whose cheeks were wet with tears. Turning his attention to Nasser, Sky offered him a similar embrace.

'How will we know when to move?' Nasser asked as he released Sky from their embrace.

'You'll know, it won't take a genius, so even you should get it.'

Both men shared a smile and Timothy realised how close the two of them were.

'The fate of Mielikuvitus seems to be in the hands of a merry band of creatures. Let's see, we do our best to save what we hold closest.'

Sky made his final comment and, before anyone could answer, he turned and transformed into the grey-coated Border Collie and sprinted off into the wasteland in front of the fort gates. The remaining unicorn men offered Nasser a nod of respect before they too transformed into their natural forms and galloped off in Sky's wake. Nasser, Timothy and Aleobe took refuge in the walls cover and watched as the distraction began.

Moving out in front of the gates, Timothy saw something impossible as Sky ran in front of a line of marching Hegel-Steffi. As the dog reached the front of the marching squad, Timothy watched as Sky seemed to split as he moved. In a heartbeat he had multiplied and there were more than a dozen Skys circling around the now frozen squad of legged-sharks.

Unable to comprehend what had happened, Timothy watched as the sickening cry of the Hegel-Steffi filled the air. In a matter of seconds scores of Hegel-Steffi raced out of the open gates to join the isolated squad and soon the Skys were forced to abandon their circling of the troops and back off into a defensive line.

'You are either brave or incredibly stupid.' A Hegel-Steffi snarled as it moved to the front of the military lines.

The centre dog transformed from dog to human and moved ahead of the line of dogs to meet the fearsome Hegel-Steffi. As Sky moved forward with grace and poise, the unicorns, majestic and bright in the darkness of Shadow Island, moved to the flanks of the line of dogs and waited.

'Come on, it's time to move.' Nasser prodded Timothy, but his attention was fixed on the terrifying Hegel-Steffi that towered over Sky in the middle of no-man's-land in front of the fort.

'Just a minute.'

The Hegel-Steffi was a fearsome sight. Even from his distance, Timothy could make out the jagged scars that peppered the shark's face and one of its eyes looked milky-white. In one hand, it carried a serrated bone that had been carved into a primitive weapon.

'We need to move,' Nasser grabbed Timothy's arm and snatched his attention back from the confrontation. 'Now!'

Unable to protest, Timothy turned from Sky and moved out of the cover they had. Hugging the wall, Nasser and Timothy moved towards the massive onyx gates that remained open.

Reaching the side of the gates, Nasser stopped them and peered around the open gates into the vast courtyard beyond.

With a nod, Nasser breached the threshold of the fort and crossed into a place where nobody from the Brightlands had been in decades. Crossing into the courtyard, the Blue Hall dominated the far side of the fort and clambered high into the sky.

'This is where we part ways.' Nasser declared as they took refuge behind a battered structure of a gatehouse. 'For what it's worth, Timothy, I may not share Sky's faith in your abilities but you a brave and tenacious boy.'

It was a curious compliment but Timothy took it on face value.

'Take care of him, Aleobe.'

'I will,' the Ecilop replied as Nasser turned and disappeared into the shadows and across the open courtyard in search of the children from Conn Uri.

Timothy was alone and, for the first time, he was left in Mielikuvitus to fend for himself. Even though Aleobe hovered by his side, there was not a lot the little Ecilop could do to help him. His heart raced in his chest as the thought of what was to come dominated his thoughts.

Not wanting to wallow in fear and apprehension, Timothy took hold of the Nosym and moved around the gatehouse. With grim determination, he stalked towards the Blue Hall.

What was left of the Hegel-Steffi inside the fort was too busy with whatever Sky's distraction had become outside the gates.

Staying in the shadows, of which there were many, Timothy made his way to the Blue Hall.

Reaching the steps leading up to the open doors of the hall, Timothy paused a moment to take in the undeniable, impressive nature of the building. Close-up the exterior walls of the Blue Hall were carved with faces and frescos telling an intricate history of events that Timothy could not comprehend.

Not wanting to risk being seen, Timothy jogged up the steps as Aleobe's wings fluttered by his ear to stay close by his side. Reaching the top of the steps as soon as Timothy stepped through the open doors, they slammed shut behind him.

Spinning to look at the doors, he realised he was trapped and ran back to force the heavy doors open.

'There's no point,' a voice declared from behind him.

'They only open and close on my command.' A second voice boomed. Timothy recognised the voice, and a shiver ran the length of his spine as he turned around.

Stepping away from the door, Timothy moved to the edge of a walkway that led down like a Greek amphitheatre to a stage dug into the floor of the hall.

Swallowing hard, Timothy looked on as the Dark Entity, a cloud of black vapour and smoke, hovered in the centre of the circular room below. The red eyes looked up at him and shone in the dim light of the hall, but it was not the Dark Entity that caught his attention the most.

Stood in front of the Dark Entity, dressed in all black, was the mysterious figure that had lunged from the shadows when Timothy had crossed through the mirror into Mielikuvitus.

'How is that possible?' Timothy gasped as he looked down at the intruder from the hallway, who turned to face him.

'My servant has been searching for a way to cross over for many years.'

'Who are you?' Timothy demanded as the burglar looked up at him, their face obscured by the balaclava.

As the Dark Entity moved to the intruder's side, Timothy realised how big it was. The Dark Entity was almost twice the height of the black clad intruder who raised their hand to pull the balaclava from their head.

Timothy could not hide the surprise and his sharp intake of breath as the intruder revealed their identity to him.

'Hello Timothy,' Dr Live, his own doctor, stood on the floor beneath him beside the creature that had haunted his nightmares for so long.

'This isn't possible,' Timothy stammered as the sense of betrayal swallowed him like a fever.

'I have long suspected what you were Timothy. When I saw the mirror in your home it was all confirmed to me.' Dr Live moved to the bottom of the circular steps and looked up at Timothy.

She looked different. Although the doctor had always had a stern and serious appearance, he knew her softer side.

As he looked down at the woman, he saw nothing of the caring doctor he trusted. All he saw was a twisted, deceitful servant of the Dark Entity.

CHAPTER TWENTY-NINE

THE DARK ENTITY

'**I**T DOESN'T HAVE TO be this way.' The Dark Entity's voice echoed. 'You have come this far fed on ideals and lies.'

Timothy felt the Entity's attention fixed on him and could not deny the unease he felt. Compared to the nightmares that had haunted him, this was far worse. For a split second, he considered reminding himself this was all a dream, as Dr Live had taught him, but as he looked at her at the bottom of the stepped auditorium, he remembered this wasn't a dream.

'You are a young boy,' Dr Live continued, her voice no longer warm and comforting. 'How can you think you can stand before the Great Dark Entity? With a view to what, destroying him?'

'They told me I was a Partum Spiritus.' Timothy choked and pulled the Nosym from his side.

'You are no Partum.' The Dark Entity boomed. 'I have seen the Partum first-hand and you, you are just a child.'

Timothy felt frustration and anger as he tightened his grip on the Nosym's wooden handle.

'Sky has trained me.' Timothy snarled through gritted teeth.

'Sky has fooled you. He has led you down a path of destruction and sacrifice for a world that means nothing to you.'

'They are my friends.'

The Dark Entity's mocking laugh filled the auditorium, and Timothy flushed with embarrassment. Both Live and the Entity stared at him as the echoes of laughter faded.

'These things are not your friend.' The Dark Entity scoffed. 'Until a few days ago, they did not exist to you.'

'Aleobe did.'

'A voice! A quiet voice that whispered in your ear when the world became a little too scary for you?' The hovering smoke and eyes mocked. 'And where has that got you?'

Dr Live moved with the grace of a stalking cat as she climbed the auditorium steps to where Timothy was standing. He watched her with caution as she drew nearer, but it was the Entity that continued to speak to him.

'You do not belong in this world. Even if you are Partum, there has been no need or place for you in Mielikuvitus. Your kind is a whisper of a memory and nothing more.'

'The business of this place has nothing to do with you,' Dr Live continued as she reached Timothy's level. 'We can offer you a way to return to your family. You can leave this place for good and be done with people who would sacrifice you for their own gain.'

'What do you mean?'

'Your so-called friends knew you would most likely fail in facing the ruler of darkness. Yet they still allowed you to come. They are not friends. They may seem that way at first but they are cowards, afraid of putting themselves in harm's way.'

Timothy watched as Dr Live directed his attention to the bottom of the auditorium where the Dark Entity waited. As he looked on, Timothy saw tendrils of smoke slither away from the Dark Entity to the side of the room. To his amazement, the smoke took form and shape until it had become a large mirror freestanding to the side of the circular stage.

'I can send you back and you can leave this place for good. To be where you belong.' The Dark Entity offered. Its words measured and calm. 'I warned you that coming here would be your end.'

'Your mother and father will miss you.' Dr Live pressed as she moved closer to him. 'Go back to them, be a family again and worry not about this place.'

Timothy could see the sense in what they were both saying. They were right that he was just a boy, too young for the battles of a strange land, but he had grown so much under Sky's guidance. His head and heart were torn and mention of his parents from the doctor, a woman he had trusted, had touched a nerve.

Both the Entity and Dr Live watched as Timothy's gaze shifted from each of them, then to the ornate mirror stood at the edge of the circular stage. The black smoke wafted from the frame, and even from where he stood, Timothy could make out the outline of his reflection in the glass.

'Why?' Timothy thought and turned his attention to the doctor. 'Why is it you are here?'

The question stunned her for a moment as she took a step backwards to compose herself.

'I have known of this place for a long time,' Dr Live confessed. 'I have sought those who have been connected to Mielikuvitus in the hope I would find a way here.'

'But how?'

'Because of me!' The Dark Entity boomed. 'I have yearned to cross the void between our worlds and, by accident, I found my way into the mind of one of your kind. It was then that I met the doctor.'

'At first I thought it was a delusion,' Dr Live explained. 'But he showed me things, places and unbelievable creatures I could never have imagined possible.'

'He tricked you.'

'No!' The doctor snapped in anger. 'He wants to connect our worlds rather than have one hidden from the other. Just think of the possibilities if we joined our worlds.'

'You're an idiot!' Timothy spat and stepped away from her. 'You say I'm the child, yet look at you! Fooled by a shadow.'

Timothy, renewed with grim determination, held out the Nosym and willed the eternal flame to emerge from the gaping mouth of the roaring lion. The flame sparked and grew until it took the form of a sword in his hands.

'You choose a fate of battle and death where I offer you peace and life?' The Dark Entity hissed from below.

'I honour my promise.' Timothy answered in defiance and grasped the flaming Nosym in both hands. 'Whatever my fate, it beats giving in to a witch and a cloud of smoke!'

Timothy fought hard to maintain an air of confidence and, judging by the look on the doctor's face, he had succeeded. He watched as the middle-aged woman turned her attention to the Dark Entity and waited for its instruction.

'So be it Timothy Scott.' The eerie voice sighed. 'Let it be known I gave you a chance to leave. Your end is of your own creation.'

Dr Live replaced the balaclava on her face and withdrew something similar to Timothy's Nosym from behind her back.

'KILL HIM!' The Dark Entity boomed and in response she attacked.

The doctor moved with incredible speed for a woman her age. She bore down on Timothy and as she did, a shield of water appeared from her left arm and a sword of rippling water emerged from the end of her weapon.

Staggering backwards, Timothy struggled to slice his Nosym through the air and watched with dismay as the flaming blade slammed into the watery shield with no effect. A hiss of steam erupted from where the fire and water met, and the doctor used her position to push him backwards, disengaging his sword from the shield.

From its position, the Dark Entity had the perfect position to watch the battle between Dr Live and Timothy.

Timothy's abilities and skill surprised it, but the Entity watched as the doctor backed him around the top level of the amphitheatre with relative ease. As their opposing blades of fire and water clashed, it filled the air with the hiss of steam each time.

Dr Live pummelled Timothy with her weapon. As she moved to deflect the sword, it was too late to realise the second attack. The shield of water slammed into his side, sending him tumbling off-balance down the steep steps of the theatre.

Feeling every step along the way, Timothy felt his body battered and bruise as he tumbled all the way to the stage floor. Dizzy from the fall, he settled his gaze and to his terror saw the burning reptilian eyes of the Dark Entity staring down at him. Fear consumed him as he scrambled across the floor from where he had landed and away from the hovering smoke and eyes.

Turning in time, he watched as Dr Live sprinted down the steps towards him, shield raised and her sword pointed out towards him.

'Never forget that a tool may change when needed.' Sky's voice whispered in his ear, although his mentor was nowhere to be seen.

Realising its meaning, Timothy closed his eyes for a second as the doctor raced towards him. Focussing once again on the eternal flame, he willed the shaft of fire that made the sword to change. As the doctor reached the penultimate step, the sword fell limp, and the flame dropped to the floor.

'Coward!' The Doctor bellowed, but no sooner had the words left her lips she realised her mistake.

Where the sword looked to have broken, it had not. Instead, Timothy had willed the flame to take on a new form and as he rotated the whip of fire above his head, she realised her mistake. Moving to halt her momentum, Timothy flicked the whip in the air as the flame arced out towards the doctor.

The nine-tails end whipped into the side of her face and burned through the material of her balaclava, charring the skin beneath. The doctor let out a yelp as the fire seared her skin and the force of the blow sent her crashing to the floor.

As she landed on the solid floor, both the shield and sword splashed into puddles of water on the floor. Gasping from the exertion of the fight, Timothy turned from the lifeless, unconscious body of Dr Live and focussed his attention on the Dark Entity hovering behind him.

'This means nothing!' It growled in anger. 'You have changed nothing. You've stopped nothing.'

'Timothy!' Sky's familiar voice shouted from high in the amphitheatre, and he turned to see both Nasser and Sky skid to the top of the steps.

As they moved to help, a wall of water erupted from the floor, blocking their path to Timothy. The sound of rushing water was drowned out by the manic laughter of the Dark Entity. To his horror, Timothy watched as it shifted its appearance and took on the smoky silhouette shape of an enormous human. Doubling in height, it towered high over Timothy.

'You should have taken my offer.'

Timothy returned the Nosym to its sword-form and prepared himself for the impending attack. As the Dark Entity lumbered forward, Timothy allowed the second flame to erupt from the mouth of the snake and span the double-edged weapon high above his head.

'You cannot kill me!' The Dark Entity roared as the fire passed through the black smoke, leaving no mark.

Filled with frustration, Timothy screamed and in response, the Nosym reacted as it had in the field the first time he had wielded it. Both ends of the flame erupted in a shower of fire and cascaded out towards the looming shadow of the Dark Entity. As the flames consumed the smoke, the Dark Entity let out a blood-curdling scream. As the flames extinguished, the smoke of the Dark Entity evaporated with them, leaving no sign of where he had been.

Confused by what had happened, unconvinced he had expelled the Dark Entity, Timothy stared in disbelief at the open space in front of him. Desperate to know what had happened, he was about to turn around when a sound caught his attention.

'Look out.' Aleobe screamed from across the room.

Turning around, he saw the doctor, the side of her face still smouldering from his attack. Propelling herself, she launched herself towards him. Releasing his grip on the Nosym, it tumbled to the floor as the doctor barrelled into him, sending them both staggering backwards across the stage of the amphitheatre.

Struggling against the woman's assault, Timothy was powerless and felt himself dragged backwards towards the mirror on the far side of the circular stage. Before he could do anything to stop their movement, the entangled pair smashed into the glass of the mirror.

As they crashed into the glass, the mirror exploded into a thousand shards of glass around them. Tumbling backwards, they did not land on the floor of the amphitheatre. As Timothy looked beyond the doctor, he saw the world close in around them as the mirror swallowed them both and sent them back home.

'No!' Was all he could muster as the void swallowed them and took them both home.

CHAPTER THIRTY

BACK TO REALITY

TIMOTHY STOOD IN THE hallway once again. The dark figure that had ambushed him now lay on the floor at the bottom of the stairs. Everything felt hazy, as if something weighed him down. As the world span around him, he tried to focus on the limp body of Dr Live at the bottom of the stairs.

When Timothy had entered the mirror and crossed to Mielikuvitus, the identity of the midnight intruder had been a mystery Now, however, he knew who it was laid at the bottom of the stairs. Staggering away from the mirror, Timothy struggled to focus on the battered body of Dr Live as she lay on the wooden floor.

Her face, which had been concealed beneath her head covering, was now exposed. The charred edges of the material exposed. The right side of her face looked red and scarred from their furious fight on Shadow Island.

Steadying himself on the ornate end of the banister, Timothy fought to free himself from the mist of dizziness and confusion. Holding the bridge of his nose, he tried to calm his breath, but a sudden movement stole his attention.

Standing almost over Dr Live, he had taken little notice of her, save for the marks from their battle. Without warning, her gloved hand grasped his ankle, and before he could respond, Timothy felt his legs pulled out from beneath him.

Falling through the air, Timothy's head smashed onto the wooden floor and stars burst into his eyes. Unable to react, the injured doctor was on him in an instant. Hampered by her injuries, she clambered up Timothy as he struggled to break free of her grasp in desperation.

Enraged and filled with hatred, the doctor was unrelenting. Timothy only hoped the crash of his fall had disturbed his parents above him. As Dr Live fought to wrap her long fingers around his neck, Timothy kicked out and pressed himself away off the bottom step. Skidding backwards across the floor, he broke free and struggled to get to his feet.

Whatever confusion had hampered the doctor had lifted enough for her to get to her knees and launch herself at Timothy.

'You've cost me everything.' She hissed, her voice harsh and frenzied.

Still unsteady, she barrelled into Timothy and sent him crashing backwards into the mounted mirror.

As she propelled Timothy backwards, he turned to see what was behind him and felt the impact before he registered what was happening. The right side of his head smashed into the main circle of mirrored glass, sending the glass cracking in an intricate spider web. Once again, stars danced in his vision and Timothy felt the warmth of blood trickling down his face.

The second crash and the sound of breaking glass had been enough to wake his parents. The hallway light illuminated, sending the pale light down the stairs, highlighting the doctor and her prey. Releasing her grip on Timothy, she turned and staggered to the front door.

As she pulled it open, she turned to look at Timothy, her part-burned face bathed in the pale moonlight.

'You have not seen the last of me; I will find a way back.' She growled through gritted teeth and as Timothy's parents descended the stairs, she disappeared into the night.

Unable to support his own weight, Timothy slid down the wall and slumped down from the impact of the blow. As unconsciousness swallowed him, the last thing Timothy saw were his mum and dad descending the stairs to help.

***

Timothy recalled nothing of the next few days until a strange smell invaded his senses. Opening his eyes, the world was unfamiliar, and he felt a wave of panic for a moment.

'It's fine Timmy,' he knew the voice, but at first couldn't place it.

'I'll get the doctor!' A male voice added and again he recognised it but couldn't put his finger on who it was.

As he moved his head, he felt waves of pain down his neck and the bright lights of the room hurt his eyes.

Turning to the side, his blurred vision focussed, and he saw the source of the voice.

'Mum?' He gasped and felt relief to see her sat beside his bed.

As his mum embraced him, a young doctor joined them in the room and introduced himself. Timothy paid little attention to the conversations between the doctor and his parents, but soon realised they were all looking at him with expectation.

'What?'

'Timmy, didn't you hear what the doctor asked?' There was a look of concern on his dad's face.

'No, sorry, I was thinking.'

'I'm Dr Singh. I was just asking what you can remember about your fall, young man?'

Timothy registered the question and felt a fog in his memory as he tried to recall what had happened. He felt tired, far more than he would expect, for having woken in the middle of the night and gone down the stairs for a drink.

Then it hit him.

Like a dam bursting, a sea of memories pushed through the fog and he saw the events in Mielikuvitus flash before his eyes in a heartbeat. Memories of Sky, Sucatraps, Aleobe, Nasser, the

Dark Entity, Shadow Island, and Dr Live all merged into a mass of memory that rendered him speechless for a moment.

'It is normal,' Dr Singh interrupted, turning his attention to Timothy's parents. 'Although the scans show no lasting injuries, an amount of memory problems is not uncommon.'

'Will he be OK though?' His mum pressed.

Timothy watched and realised his dad was not listening to the doctor but was, instead, focussed on Timothy. Meeting his gaze, there was a knowing look on his father's face that made him feel rather uncomfortable.

Closing his eyes to avoid the quizzical look, Timothy soon found sleep again and wandered his dreams in search of many things.

Timothy remained in hospital for three more days, observed by a multitude of doctors and nurses, until they were happy he could go home. Although his parents remained at his side in shifts, Timothy had searched for any sign of Aleobe. There had been nothing and as his mum packed what few belongings he had with him, there was an empty and lonely feeling hanging in the air.

As Dr Singh handed a bag of medication to his mum, the doctor offered Timothy a hurried farewell and disappeared to tend to another patient on the ward. Glad to be freed from the confines of the hospital, Timothy walked with caution along the corridors and out of the main doors of the hospital. He was happy to find his dad waiting in the car park.

The familiar black people-carrier sat idling in the car park and as his mum pulled open the sliding door, Timothy couldn't help but smile as he saw Cathy and Aiden sat in the back waiting for him.

'Thanks little bro!' Aiden beamed as he pointed to his watch. 'You got me out of school.'

Sliding into his seat, Timothy rested his head against the headrest and felt a strange comfort at being surrounded by his family again.

As his mum closed the door, he opened his eyes as his sister took hold of his arm and hugged him from her seat.

'Missed you!' She said and rested her head against him.

'What do you say we get something to eat as a bit of a celebration at Timothy coming home?'

Nobody in the car disagreed, and the family spent the rest of the afternoon enjoying each other's company until the tiredness once again threatened to swallow Timothy. Sensing it was time to leave, they got back into the car and returned home.

Stepping through the front door, Timothy felt relief as they shut the door behind him, securing him back at home. As he walked along the hallway, he could not help but glance at the mirror, somehow in the hope he would see Aleobe fluttering somewhere near to him, but he saw nothing.

In the cracked glass, all he could see were dozens of reflections of himself staring at him from the other side. The reflection matched his movements and there was nothing to tell him his path to Mielikuvitus existed anymore.

'I'll get that sorted,' his dad declared as he hoisted the mirror from the wall. 'I know you're tired. It's up to you if you stay downstairs or go to bed.'

'Just want to go to bed,' Timothy muttered as he climbed up the stairs, supporting himself on the banister. 'I want to get some sleep.'

Timothy was dejected and very much alone as he made his way to his room. Feeling his dad's eyes watching him as he climbed the stairs, he was desperate to hear Aleobe. At the top of the stairs, there was nothing but silence.

Resigning himself to silence, Timothy moved to ready himself for bed.

CHAPTER THIRTY-ONE

THE CELLAR

As TIMOTHY GOT HIMSELF ready for bed, his dad joined him in the bathroom.

'Can I talk to you?' His dad asked as he replaced the dressing on Timothy's temple.

'What's up?'

'You've been quiet all evening, like something's bothering you.' His dad offered as he threw the bloodstained dressing in the bin and secured the replacement against his skin. 'Is there anything you want to talk about?'

Timothy had always felt closest to his dad, for all his seriousness he had always shared the flights of fancy from his imagination as he had grown up. His dad had always been the one to encourage him to embrace what he called his uniqueness at being different.

Looking at his dad's reflection in the bathroom mirror, it was hard to hold back the tears that came with the undeniable self-doubt he was feeling.

'Whatever it is you can tell me, you know that.' His dad soothed. 'I won't push you, you can come to me in your own time, but you need to know you're not alone.'

'It doesn't always feel that way.' Timothy sighed and dropped his gaze to the sink.

Timothy chanced a glance at the mirror in the slightest hope he would see Aleobe's reflection somewhere in the room, but still, as it had been for days, there was nothing.

Gerard Scott watched his son with curiosity. He saw his eyes scanning the reflection in the mirror as if searching for something he could not find. The look on his son's face was something he could relate to, and he remembered being around the same age and feeling the weight of the world on his shoulders.

'I want to show you something,' he announced, snatching Timothy's attention back from searching the mirror. 'Come with me.'

Consumed with curiosity, Timothy dried his hands on the towel and followed his dad out of the bathroom. Without a word, they descended the staircase and Timothy realised the mirror had gone from the wall at the bottom of the stairs.

Before he could ask what had happened to the mirror, his dad moved to the kitchen and removed a small key from the top of the doorframe where the cellar entrance stood.

The cellar was a place they never allowed the children to go. The key had always been secreted on top of the doorframe and while Aiden and Timothy could reach it they had never ventured down the dark steps beneath the house. There had never been a need to go down there, and both his parents had always been very insistent. They told the children it was filled with dangerous things they were best to stay away from.

Checking around, Timothy watched as his dad slipped the key into the hole and twisted it around, unlocking the door. Pulling it open, he turned to look at Timothy and waited for him to walk through the door.

'I know what's going on,' his dad explained as he closed and locked the door behind them. 'There's a lot you're holding back. A lot of things you think I won't understand, but I need you to know something.'

The stairs were lit by a dim bulb that hung from the ceiling and as they reached the bottom, his dad switched on the light in the main cellar room.

Much to Timothy's surprise, the room was empty. The floor was dusty, and what shelves there were sat covered in a thick layer of dust. Turning to his father, his brow furrowed as he tried to understand what his dad was trying to show him.

'I thought you said there were dangerous things down here?' Timothy asked as he looked around the room.

'Sometimes we do our best to protect you. It may not always be right, but I hope your realise now why I did it?'

It made no sense to Timothy what his dad was saying. He watched as his dad walked across the empty cellar to the far wall. Awash with curiosity, he watched as his dad wiped his hand over the dusty brick as if searching for something in particular.

Seeming to have found what he was looking for, Timothy watched as his dad brushed off one particular brick in the centre of the wall and then pushed it. To his surprise, the brick moved under his dad's pressure and disappeared. With a loud *crack,* a whole third of the wall to his dad's right moved aside and reveal a room beyond.

'What's happening, dad?'

His question went unanswered and his dad beckoned for him to follow as he ducked underneath the low arch, now exposed as the wall had slid to the side. The room beyond was pitch-black and Timothy could see nothing. Shuffling with uneasy steps, he followed until he felt the pressure of his father's hand on his stomach stopping him mid-step.

'Where are we?'

'This is the reason you have never been allowed down here, Tim,' his dad explained. 'You forget the one thing I have always told you.'

Before finishing his sentence, the room was bathed in light and Timothy found himself stood in a room filled with mirrors. Someone had mounted mirrors of every shape and type to the four walls and they reflected the spotlights mounted on the ceiling. On the far wall, Timothy noted the cracked hallway mirror resting on the floor.

'I know why you pretend that you can't remember anything. Your mother told me about your hesitation when the doctor asked.'

'I'm not pretending.' Timothy defended.

'But you can remember,' his dad interrupted and took hold of his shoulders, turning him to face him. 'You remember everything, but you doubt what you are remembering.'

Timothy allowed himself to be guided across the room by his dad until he was standing in front of the broken mirror from the hallway. As his father turned him to face the mirror, he felt his father's breath as he whispered in his ear.

'Everything you remember, all those fantastic things you doubt are real,' his dad pointed to the mirror. 'They are real, Tim. They always have been.'

Looking at the angled mirror, Timothy saw his own reflection and there, perched on his shoulder, was the familiar image of Aleobe.

'Mielikuvitus is a place that has existed for our family for longer than you would believe.'

Stepping back from Timothy, his dad pointed to the rest of the mirrors covering the walls and as Timothy turned around, each one changed from his reflection to a windowed view to the Brightlands of Mielikuvitus. Tears welled in his eyes as the fog of doubt and insecurity evaporated in a heartbeat.

'You're not the only one to have walked the lands, my son.'

His dad's words were inconsequential and fell on deaf ears as Timothy felt relief at seeing the pastel-coloured trees wafting in a breeze he could not feel. For this first time since returning, he felt comfort in his surroundings.

In a mirror to his side, a slight movement caught Timothy's attention. As he turned, he saw Sky and Sucatraps walking across the grassland towards the banks of the Rainbow River. As the pair were deep in conversation, they seemed oblivious to Timothy's gaze upon them.

'Welcome back.' Aleobe declared, as he waved at Timothy from inside the mirror. 'You should be proud of him Gerard, he's done you proud.'

Timothy's mouth was wide as he turned to look at his dad standing next to him.

'You know him?'

'I do son, he was there when you were born and I asked him to look after you from that moment.'

Timothy hugged his dad tight and allowed the tears to flow from his eyes.

Surrounded by the panoramic view of Mielikuvitus, Timothy realised how much he had grown. The dangers he had overcome and things he had faced filled him with a sense of pride. That pride was reflected in the tight embrace from his dad.

Timothy felt, for the first time, he was worthy of the title Partum Spiritus.

As father and son hugged, united by the commonality, neither of them noticed the steady flow of black mist from the mirror from the hallway. As the thin mist rolled from the cracked corner of the mirror, the familiar burning red eyes of the Dark Entity appeared in the glass.

It hovered their silent, watching the two of them in the cellar.

MORE ADVENTURE

His sister kidnapped. An ominous rose calling him back through the mirror. Can Timothy save his sister before an ancient creature claims her as its own...forever?

TIMOTHY SCOTT: TORN MOUNTAINS

<u>**GET YOUR COPY NOW - SCAN THE CODE BELOW**</u>

OR ELSE VISIT **TOBEY-ALEXANDER.COM/BTM**

H IS SISTER KIDNAPPED. HIS family under threat. Timothy Scott must once again return to the world behind the mirror.

Having faced the Dark Entity in battle Timothy had thought his time in the world behind the mirror was over. When his younger sister disappears he feels a wave of dread as he discovers a black rose sticking through the glass of the broken antique mirror. Fearing the worst, Timothy must return to his friends and call on them to help him save his sister.

Timothy soon finds himself going back through the mirror but things are not as he left them. While the Dark Entity's reign of fear has subsided, a new danger has grown and a long-forgotten beast from the labyrinth beneath the Torn Mountains holds his sister prisoner. Aided by an unexpected ally, Timothy must once again face his fears if he has any hope of saving his sister and bringing her home.

REVIEW

HELP OTHERS DISCOVER TIMOTHY'S adventures by leaving me a review on Amazon. I love to hear what my readers think and personally read every review!

Printed in Great Britain
by Amazon